"DID YOU COME DOWN HERE TO BUY SOME . . . underwear? I have some beautiful stock," she pointed out, enjoying how uncomfortable the subject made him. "Is there a . . . wife?" She held her breath, strangely relieved when he shook his head. "Girlfriend?"

"I didn't come to buy underwear, for me or anyone else," he assured her, taking a step into the only available space in the entire room.

"If you don't want underwear, how about a bathrobe?"

"No, thank you." He took another step.

"Nightwear?" she squeaked.

"I don't wear any."

"Oh, my," she whispered.

His gaze slid slowly over her, from her low neckline, to her short hemline, and everywhere in between.

Suddenly the stuffy scientist didn't seem so stuffy, but the room sure did. "What *did* you come for?" she asked, her voice low and trembly.

He took one more step, which brought him within a fraction of an inch from Trisha.

"Hunter?"

"Hmm?"

"Why are you here?"

A wordless sound of frustrated humor came from him. "I haven't the foggiest," he muttered before he covered her mouth with his.

WHAT ARE *LOVESWEPT* ROMANCES?

They are stories of true romance and touching emotion. We believe those two very important ingredients are constants in our highly sensual and very believable stories in the LOVE-SWEPT line. Our goal is to give you, the reader, stories of consistently high quality that may sometimes make you laugh, sometimes make you cry, but are always fresh and creative and contain many delightful surprises within their pages.

Most romance fans read an enormous number of books. Those they truly love, they keep. Others may be traded with friends and soon forgotten. We hope that each LOVESWEPT romance will be a treasure—a "keeper." We will always try to publish

LOVE STORIES YOU'LL NEVER FORGET
BY AUTHORS YOU'LL ALWAYS REMEMBER

The Editors

Loveswept ® 885

THE HARDER THEY FALL

JILL SHALVIS

BANTAM BOOKS
NEW YORK · TORONTO · LONDON · SYDNEY · AUCKLAND

THE HARDER THEY FALL

A Bantam Book / April 1998

ISBN 0-553-44623-1

Published simultaneously in the United States and Canada

Bantam Books are published by Bantam Books, a division of Bantam Dou-
bleday Dell Publishing Group, Inc. Its trademark, consisting of the words
"Bantam Books" and the portrayal of a rooster, is Registered in U.S.
Patent and Trademark Office and in other countries. Marca Registrada.
Bantam Books, 1540 Broadway, New York, New York 10036.

PRINTED IN THE UNITED STATES OF AMERICA

OPM   10 9 8 7 6 5 4 3 2 1

For David, and the
best ten years of my life

AUTHOR'S NOTE

I'm often asked where I get my ideas. For this story, the hero and the heroine have a rather unconventional start—they meet when she falls on him through a hole in the ceiling while he's standing before the toilet. Funny, but not very romantic. Not too long ago, I was at a writers' meeting. In the bathroom, far above me, there was a hole. It flapped open, revealing a dark, yawning space. As I sat there contemplating this hole, I wondered what would happen if a really, really gorgeous man fell through it. One didn't, darn it, but a story was born.

ONE

"Only you, Aunt Eloise, could haunt me from the dead."
Hunter sighed and reread the note he'd gotten from his
great-aunt's attorney. The lighthearted tone of the note
sounded so like Eloise had in life, he had to smile. But
the amusement drained as the implications of the message sank in.

Well, I'm finally dead, she wrote. *And while you might
be breathing a sigh of relief, it's a little premature. We rarely
saw eye to eye; me, an old woman intent on love and laughter,
and you intent on little else but your work. Yet I always knew
you loved me. It showed every time you had to save me from
some financial scheme or another. I owe you so much money, I
lost track long ago.*

"There's a surprise," Hunter muttered.

*And I know, even grumbling as you no doubt are, you'd
never let me pay you back anyway. So I'm leaving you my
place.*

Hunter blanched. "No. Not the duplex."

*I love that place, as you know. Yes, yes, as cosmetic value
goes, it needs a tad of work.*

Hunter shook his head and snorted.

But if I'd left it to your mother, we both know she'd have sold it and blown all the proceeds within a week. I know this is an unwanted burden and an imposition for someone who has been nothing but kind to me, but please, Hunter, if you do nothing else, concentrate on something other than your work for a time. It'll be good for you. Take care, Hunter, and remember, mad as you are right now, I love you with all my heart.

Her signature was the same as always, wide and bold. *Great-Aunt Eloise.*

Hunter looked up and stared in displeasure at the rambling, creaking duplex he'd just inherited. The old pile, although charming with its chipped brick front and white-paned windows, looked as if it was on its last legs. Shutters hung crookedly on both levels. Paint peeled off in massive chunks.

A mess, he decided, and he most definitely did not like messes. Any one of his lab techs, whom he regularly terrorized without meaning to, would attest to that.

Someone in the upstairs apartment had a stereo blaring out country blues, rattling the already rattled-looking windows. Probably the same someone singing off-key, loudly.

Because he knew the bottom apartment was empty, he let himself in. Large, airy rooms. Perfect size, very imperfect condition. Sneezing, he shook his head. Dust covered everything, including the various pieces of furniture his aunt had left. Art Deco mixed with cheap antique reproductions. Hunter shuddered.

What would he do with such a place? Demolition seemed appropriate. Yet he couldn't stay forever in the small hotel NASA had provided. But a house would only remind him, cruelly, of his own failings, and of a pain much better buried in his past. His dear, sweet aunt had meant well by leaving him this place, but he couldn't possibly keep it.

Two bathrooms. And after all the tea he'd consumed at the luncheon, it couldn't hurt to check the plumbing. He hated those obligatory events, designed for the sole purpose of charming rich women out of their money, all in the name of research. But much as he disliked them, he always attended. As head of his department he had no choice, plus he had the dubious honor of being called the Devil of the entire floor.

In other words, he could charm the last penny out of a miser, especially when the goal was to fund his research.

Upstairs, the country music still rocked the building, disturbing his thoughts. At least the singing had stopped. But he'd no sooner stepped into a bathroom and unzipped than a creak had him glancing up. Above him, the ceiling panel lifted and two curious brown eyes peered down at him.

Indignation left him stunned, just for a second. Then the panel groaned warningly, and even he knew what that meant. Before he could react, a shrieking, laughing female landed on him, hitting him square in the chest.

Instinctively, he caught her, then tightened his tenuous hold. "What the—"

"Oh, my!" the wriggling mass of woman exclaimed, pushing hair from her face. She blinked up at him. "Oh, my."

Hunter considered himself a calm man, rational and even-tempered at all times. He had nerves of steel, courtesy of years of researching, preparing, and flying experiments on NASA missions most people didn't even know existed. But nothing about him felt particularly calm and rational now, not when he stood before a toilet with his pants unzipped, holding a woman he didn't know. Turning, he unceremoniously dumped her on the hideous black-and-white-checkered linoleum. From above, Hank Williams continued to croon at an ear-shattering decibel level.

The woman let out another startled little laugh and straightened, turning toward him with wide eyes. "Oh, my goodness."

Her vocabulary certainly wasn't anything to remark on, but her manners were. He opened his mouth but nothing came out except his own hot breath, so he closed it again, positively speechless.

It didn't matter, she apparently didn't have the same problem.

"Oh, no," she cried, brushing white plaster dust off her short, tight black vinyl skirt. "Look . . . I got this all dirty. They'll never take it back now." Sighing dramatically, she looked at him. "I run a boutique, you see. And I just got this great shipment, but I don't think this works, not really. Now, maybe if it were red . . ." She bit her lip, deciding, while Hunter just stood there, flabbergasted. "No, not even if it were red," she decided.

"Who are you?" he managed to say.

Smiling, she stuck out a hand. "Trisha Malloy. I live upstairs. Did you just rent this place?"

"Not exactly." He tipped his head back. Yep, the hole was still there, gaping. She'd definitely fallen out of there. "Do you always spy on people when they're in the bathroom?"

"Oh, no!" she assured him, putting her hands over her chest for emphasis. White dust on her hands, probably more plaster dust, left imprints on the leopard-print crop top she wore. "It's just that I didn't expect anyone.

This apartment's been empty for some time. *Wow*. I guess that leak we had in the last rain left the floor more unstable than I thought." She studied the hole. "There used to be a teeny, tiny, little hole I could peek through. I just wanted to be sure you weren't an intruder." Then she looked him up and down. "But you wouldn't be, not all dressed up like that."

That this woman talking to him had large, melting brown eyes and long brown hair the color of a doe's, on a face meant for an artist's canvas, all attached to a nifty little compact body that could tempt the gods meant nothing. She was insane.

"I'm so glad the place finally got rented. Poor Eloise," the woman said. "I miss her. She was worried her nephew would let her down and sell the house. Told me he was a stuffy scientist."

Space scientist, he thought wearily. Not stuffy.

"And that he worked in NASA, hiding himself from life in some laboratory, studying Mars, of all things. *Mars*," she repeated with disdainful emphasis. "But she wanted him to take this place and learn to enjoy life."

Enjoy life. He felt no need to explain that he'd lived wild and out of control his entire childhood, thanks to his equally wild and out-of-control parents, and planned never to do it again.

Now the crazy lady smiled, and it was a dazzler. "Everyone should do that," she said. "Enjoy themselves. Don't you think?"

Hunter could only stare. The woman plucked at the provocative top that hugged her every curve, bobbing her head gently to the beat of the music, which was beginning to give him a headache.

"You know," she said, looking down, "this isn't right for me either."

Lacking anything to say that would make much sense, Hunter's gaze followed her movements, and stuck like glue to her breasts. Amazingly, he felt the stir of something he didn't often experience—pure lust.

"I'm afraid that entire shipment is going to have to be returned," she said ruefully, still looking down at herself in that incredibly tight skirt. "Ugh, it's awfully snug on these hips of mine."

Her hips were perfect, and curved just right on top of surprisingly long legs. Hunter dragged his gaze up to meet hers, shocked at how he'd reacted to this strange woman who'd just fallen on him out of nowhere.

"It's a shame," she said sadly. "All that freighting cost, but I just can't, in good conscience, sell something I don't believe in." Again that stunning smile, the one that had Hunter's stomach tightening. "So . . . what's your name?"

Finally, he found his voice. "I'm the stuffy—er, space scientist. Dr. Hunter Adams."

"Eloise's nephew?" Her smile never faltered. "Well, Dr. Space Scientist, I'm proud of you, you didn't sell."

She looked immensely relieved, so much so that he almost felt guilty as he muttered, "I still might."

"Oh." The joy just disappeared from her face. "I see." Quietly, with surprising dignity, she moved to the door. "Well, then. I can only hope you'll change your mind."

Too many broken promises in Hunter's past had left him with a major distaste for making any more. He never made promises. Never, but he was fair to a fault. "I'm sorry. But if you have to move, I can assure you I'll give you plenty of notice."

Those red lips curved, but her eyes still looked sad. "I won't be moving, Dr. Adams."

"No?" Her confidence irked him. So did the way the hands on her hips emphasized their lushness trapped in black vinyl. "You will if I sell."

"No, I won't," she said sweetly but firmly. "Eloise gave me a lifetime lease."

He sputtered, actually sputtered. He'd given speeches to entire governments, his staff numbered in the hundreds. He'd been in space three times. Yet this woman tied up his tongue with just a look. It was humiliating.

So, he realized after the enigmatic woman had spun and left, was the fact that the entire time he'd stood talking to her, his zipper had been down.

A day later Trisha sat in the middle of her living-room floor, muddling through her bookkeeping for Leather and Lace. At her feet were three boxes of her latest shipment from New York that she still had to go through and approve. Rock music blared from her stereo, an attempt on her part to lighten the unavoidable "paying bills" mood.

"For someone who sells underwear," she muttered to Duff, the black cat who lay sprawled over her spreadsheets, "I sure do generate a lot of paperwork."

Duff actually summoned enough energy to lift his head and look at her.

"I know, I know." She stroked Duff's sleek fur. "It's a living." Now she grinned, a little wickedly. "And such a fun one." Raised by her military uncle and church-crazed aunt, fun hadn't been in her vocabulary until all too recently. "If only Aunt Hilda could see me now."

Duff seemed to match her grin, and Trisha laughed. "Can you imagine the look on that saintly woman's face at the thought of her poor, orphaned niece selling lingerie? She'd have sprayed me with holy water and prayed for my soul for a month."

Well, she wasn't a frightened little mouse anymore, Trisha reminded herself. Living life to its fullest was her only goal—difficult as that creed might be. Letting loose with things such as her wardrobe didn't come easy after years of being repressed. It didn't come easy to remember she was free to think and feel what she wanted. But she would do it. She would create a full life for herself, and she would enjoy it.

Duff yawned and stretched, scattering a couple of invoices. Tired of working and worrying about money, Trisha lay back on the floor. She stretched, too, staring at the high-beamed ceiling, the plaster-coated brick walls. For a place nearly a century old, it was in remarkable shape. And she loved it beyond reason.

Maybe because she'd been forced to move nearly every year of her life while growing up. Maybe because she'd never been allowed to put down roots. It could have been a lot of things she wasn't willing to think about now—whatever the reason, she didn't ever want to leave.

But now she might have to.

For the first time all day Trisha allowed herself to think of the death of her landlord. Sadness filled her, as did the self-pity she'd managed to keep at bay.

Selfish as it was, Trisha had to face the bitter fact— Eloise's death might mean the end of her time in the place where she'd been the happiest since . . . ever. Sitting up, she pulled the closest box toward her and opened it.

Red silk and satin spilled out as she held up a gorgeous teddy, trimmed in delicate lace. Perfect for

Leather and Lace. Perfect for her customers, all with someone to please. She forced her chin up. Just because she didn't have someone special in her life didn't mean she couldn't appreciate pretty things. Besides, she didn't want someone in her life. Freedom. That's what she wanted.

Duff, sensing her somber mood, climbed into her lap and pressed his head into her palm. Obliging, she scratched behind his ears, smiling a little when he started that rumbling purr she loved so much. Silly, she told herself, that a woman of twenty-five could feel her life had just begun, but it was true. Because of that, she had to live each moment to its fullest.

And now Hunter Adams wanted to change all that, force her to move once again. Just the thought had her unreasonably panicked. He had not been what she expected, not at all. A stuffy scientist, Eloise had told her, which had conjured up pictures of an old, graying man. But he'd been nothing like that. Young, built, with a powerful grace that spoke of great physical conditioning, but definitely not old or graying.

A sharp rap on the door had her lifting her head in surprise. No, she thought, rising from the floor to face the man she'd been thinking of, Hunter Adams was nothing like what she'd expected.

Briefly, she wished she'd changed after her workout, or had at least pulled on a sweatshirt over the revealing aerobic outfit she wore. Then she reminded herself that she no longer cared what people thought of her.

"Hello." He had to shout over the music, and he didn't look too happy about it. His elegant attire—dark silk dress shirt and perfectly draped matching trousers—which she was sure he'd consider casual, only succeeded in making him all the more masculine. So did that sun-kissed blond hair and serious expression that highlighted patrician, yet rugged features. Those clear green eyes narrowed in annoyance as the music shifted, speeding up in beat and increasing in volume, but he said nothing, just placed his hands on his hips and waited.

Ah, a man used to being in charge. This was likely to get good. Amused, Trisha moved to the stereo, complying with his silent demand. Okay, maybe the scientist could be a little stuffy, a little overbearing, if one let him. She could only imagine how he terrified his peers, but not her. Nope, never again would she let herself be terrified or intimidated by anyone.

Besides, it was hard to be intimidated by a man she'd seen with his pants unzipped.

As the music lowered in decibel level, so did his eyebrows. "How can you think with it so loud?"

"I can think just fine." Crossing her arms, she watched as Duff stepped over her scattered papers and books to check out the new stranger. Without hesitation, the purring cat rubbed his head and body around Hunter's legs, and a cloud of black cat hair rose.

Trisha bit her lip and kept her eyes on Hunter's, hoping he wouldn't notice. No such luck.

"Your cat sheds."

The disapproval was apparent and Trisha's amusement abruptly faded. She'd had enough disapproval to last a lifetime. Besides, any man who didn't like cats, no matter how devastatingly handsome, didn't belong in her apartment. "Was there something I could help you with?"

At her chilly tone, he glanced at her, something in his eyes catching her attention. Not humor, it couldn't be, not in Dr. Hunter Adams's eyes. Yet there it was.

Bending in one easy motion, he scooped up the cat,

folded his arms around his considerable body, and scratched Duff behind the ears in his exact favorite spot.

She could hear Duff's purr from across the room, and despite herself, Trisha melted on the spot.

"Planning on dropping through any ceilings today?" he asked evenly.

She'd never been one to hold a grudge, especially with a man who could charm her cat *and* laugh at himself. "Not today, no. What brings you out here?" A suspicion gripped her, seized her gut. "You're not here with a 'For Sale' sign, are you?"

"No." He put Duff down, and the cat immediately rolled onto his back at Hunter's feet, obviously hoping for a friendly scratch on the belly. "But you must have a hole in your floor from . . . where you fell. I thought I should look at it."

Unable to help it, Trisha grinned. "I never did apologize for that."

"Do you make that a habit, spying on men in bathrooms?"

Was that a faint blush in his cheeks? It couldn't be, Trisha decided. Nothing would embarrass Dr. Adams. "Not often," she replied with a little laugh. "And I am sorry if I startled you."

"Startled?" He shook his head. "You damn near killed me."

The man was huge. His wide shoulders and powerful build left no doubt that he was in excellent shape. "I'm not all that heavy," she protested, scooping Duff up when he walked her way, looking for more attention.

"Heavy, no," he admitted. "But that vinyl was slippery. You're lucky I didn't drop you right in the toilet."

A giggle escaped her at the memory of the indescribable look on Hunter's face yesterday, but it quickly backed up in her throat when she watched his gaze roam down the length of the two-piece teal bodysuit she wore.

"No vinyl today, I see."

There'd been a time when she'd been made to wear nothing but school uniforms, then the most conservative of business clothes while attending college. Now she dressed for herself, and no one else, and if that meant she went a little wild sometimes, what did it matter? She liked it. "No, no vinyl today." Because she knew he disapproved of her, she didn't bother to explain that she didn't like vinyl either.

He cleared his throat. "About the hole—"

Her phone rang, and Trisha hesitated. It was late Sunday afternoon and that could mean only one person. Her uncle Victor. No way would she answer it this week. No way would he make her feel guilty or depressed about her life and how she'd chosen to lead it.

Ring, ring, ring.

No way, she repeated to herself as her hand itched to stop the ringing. Not even if the man was still grieving . . . oh, hell. She was stubborn, not heartless. Shoving both the cat and the red lace teddy she still held at the baffled doctor, she whirled for the phone.

Hunter stared down at the burden in his hands. Duff immediately demanded, loudly, to be released, and Hunter let him go. But the soft, satiny thing . . . God.

He could picture her in it, all that thick, flowing hair behind her, shimmering eyes, that tight body filling out the silk.

What was it she'd called him? The stuffy scientist? He was well aware that he'd come off formal and reserved. But she'd unnerved the hell out of him in the bathroom the day before, and now he was flustered beyond belief from just fingering the woman's underwear.

What was it about this chatty, crazy lady that did that to him?

His department would enjoy this. The Devil himself, flustered by a wild pixie of a woman who didn't know how to dress, whose apartment looked like a cyclone had hit it. Who sold *underwear* for a living.

Order. After having grown up in this very sort of environment, with a flighty actress for a mother and a wanderlust-struck artist for a father, Hunter liked order in his life. Apparently, Trisha didn't know the meaning of the word. Unwanted memories stung him. How many times had he been willing to sacrifice his needs for the people in his life, only to have them throw those needs back in his face?

Well, no more. He wanted organization, control, routine, and he'd get it. But being here, with this woman who somehow drove him to forget what he wanted and needed, was dangerous. His insides tightening uncomfortably, he straightened and set down the lingerie. He needed out of this house, badly.

"They hung up before I got there." Trisha replaced the receiver and looked immensely relieved. She sighed deeply, and in doing so, brought his attention to her bare stomach. Her flat, tanned, bare stomach.

"You mentioned your lease before," Hunter said carefully, a little desperately.

She stiffened. "What about it?"

"I'll buy it out," he said recklessly.

Her expression didn't change. "Absolutely not."

TWO

"Think about it," Hunter suggested while hopelessness coursed through his veins. What if she wouldn't leave? "I'll make a very generous offer."

"No." Trisha lifted her shoulders, stretching her top high on her ribs, outlining the firm curves of her breasts. "You're stuck with me."

He had to take a deep breath and turn away. Concentrating on the mess that was her home helped. That is, until he focused in on the red and black satin teddies strewn over her couch. Of their own accord, his fingers reached out and scooped one up, the satin rubbing sensuously over his skin.

Not your type, he had to repeat to himself, over and over again, like a mantra.

It didn't work.

Following a method he'd perfected long ago when something or someone upset him, he closed his eyes and mentally counted to ten, waiting for the visions of this insane woman wearing nothing but silk to go away.

"What are you doing?" he heard her ask, but he just kept counting. *Four, five, six* . . .

"Are you . . . counting?"

Moving around him, she stared at him with a mix of curiosity and amusement. "You are. You're counting." She laughed, a light musical sound that had him grating his teeth.

"*Seven.*"

He hadn't realized he'd spoken out loud, but she laughed again. "Dr. Adams, you can't be serious."

"Show me the hole," he managed to say, rather politely, he thought.

But she just kept that infuriating smile in place and didn't move. "You know what? I think you just play at this stodgy, superiority thing to intimidate people."

"What?"

"It probably works with your . . . whatever you scientists call your assistants," she went on, undisturbed by his glare. "But here, Dr. Adams, in my apartment, we're equals."

"I own the place." Where the hell had that come from? *I own the place.* Good Lord, he sounded just like the intolerant jerk she thought he was. "I mean—"

"I know what you mean." She turned from him, entirely without the show of temper he expected, and sauntered back over to her stereo in her teal workout clothes that so nicely encased her—

The stereo blared even louder as Trisha turned it up with a flick of her wrist, her face carefully devoid of that carefree expression he'd come to expect from her.

He'd hurt her feelings. "Trisha."

There was no way he could hear himself think, much less have a conversation over the music, which he knew she'd turned up on purpose. "Trisha—"

Smiling sweetly, she moved past him, grabbing the teddy from his hand as she went. The satiny material slid slowly through his fingers. Her thick hair brushed his arm.

He still couldn't think, but now it wasn't the music that echoed in his brain. Nope. It was the scent of this irritating, sexy woman floating over him. Taking a deep breath, he tried again, knowing he had to straighten this matter out. "Trisha."

No one could hear a thing over that noise, and certainly not Ms. Malloy, who was obviously ignoring him. "Trisha, please. Could you turn that down?"

She didn't look at him, just started singing as she scooped her shipment off the couch one item at a time, draping them over her arm.

"*Trisha?*"

"Sorry," she sang out with a smile, flipping her hair over her shoulder. "Can't hear you."

Moved by a temper he didn't know he possessed, Hunter stalked to the door. Women, he reminded himself harshly, rarely fitted into his life, and this was proof positive. "Forget it," he muttered. "I'll send a contractor."

Once in the fresh air, free of the bewitching scent of that woman, Hunter sighed gratefully. He'd nearly tossed his good intentions aside and done what his body seemed to be aching to do—kiss the living daylights out of her. But he'd made it out safe, without making a fool of himself, close as it had been. After all, his self-control rivaled the best of the best.

So why then, he wondered a bit desperately as he drove to his lab, couldn't he get the sight of Trisha Malloy, his new and irritating tenant with the soft smile and wild ways, out of his head?

Hunter sent a contractor *and* a cleaning crew to his new duplex, and then had dreams about the place every night for a week. Maybe nightmares was a better word, for the place seemed to obsess him. Or rather, the tenant in it did. What was it about the woman who dressed so outrageously? Was it her huge, sweet eyes and generous, smiling mouth, which seemed to clash with the image she projected?

Maybe it was even baser than that, nothing more than her husky voice and incredibly lush body.

Whatever it was, he had to admit, he was fascinated in a way he hadn't been in a long time.

He dropped his elbows to his desk and rubbed his temples.

"Darling, you *are* going to sell it, aren't you?"

He glanced up and mentally groaned at the sight of his mother. "How did you get past security?"

"*Our World*, of course." Gloria Ann Whitfield Adams smiled and patted her sleek, red bob. She had red lips, red nails, and wore a hot red dress with four-inch heels in fire-engine red to match. "The entire front desk downstairs claims never to have missed an episode. I signed their uniforms."

Hunter had a clearance of the highest level, and security scrutinized him every morning. His mother just waltzed right in. "Good thing the Cold War is over."

"Don't be angry, darling. A television star always attracts attention."

His mother, a diva of daytime for nearly thirty years, the same woman who had made and lost more fortunes than Hunter could count, sent him an innocent smile.

He sighed deeply at that smile, knowing he was in for it. "I'm really busy today."

"Nonsense," she declared. "You can never be too busy for your mother." Casually, she ran her fingers over his latest flight experiment, a one-eighth-scale steel model of the telescope he'd take with him on his next space-shuttle mission—the telescope that would allow him to study the strange and unusual gathering of air molecules one hundred miles into Mars's atmosphere. Under her questing and not too gentle fingers, the delicate eyepiece gave slightly.

For peace of mind, he scooted the model back. He could ask her not to touch, could tell her that this latest multibillion-dollar project just might make it possible for mankind eventually to take a trip to Mars, but he didn't bother.

It had no place in her whirlwind world, therefore, she couldn't care less.

"So," she said casually, which put his guard up instantly, since nothing was *ever* casual with Gloria, "when do you sell?"

"Sell what?"

She sighed the sigh of a martyr dealing with a half-wit. "That monstrosity that Aunt Eloise left you. It's worth a fortune."

"Is it?"

"You know that it is. It's in a high-dollar district on nearly an acre of land." Perfectly made-up green eyes batted at him.

"Big loss again this weekend in Vegas, huh?"

Her lips tightened imperceptibly. "Why do you assume it was me? It could have been your father, you know. The way he haunts Paris as if just being there were going to give him that famous reputation he's always chasing. It's humiliating, if you ask me. Everyone knows artists don't become well-known until they're dead. And he's far too stubborn to die."

This conversation was definitely not a new one. His parents, married twenty years, divorced ten years, and now living together, couldn't seem to decide if they loved or hated each other. It never failed to confuse him. "Mother—"

"If you sold that place, it would be only fair for you to divide the profit. Eloise was my favorite aunt, you know."

He laughed. His mother and Eloise had barely tolerated each other. "Now I *know* you lost last weekend. How much?"

"It's not funny." She sank into the nearest chair, tossed her head back dramatically, and covered her eyes with her hands. "I came to throw myself on your mercy and you're laughing at me."

"How much do you need?" he asked more gently, sighing as he glanced at his watch. Five minutes until his staff meeting, and if he didn't get rid of her before then, he would hear about it for the rest of the week. He'd never understand why his personal life riveted his staff members so.

His mother smiled at him, her eyes shining with warmth and affection. "You're so good to me, Hunter. You always have been."

He got out his checkbook.

"What are you going to do with the place?"

"Maybe I'll live in it."

His mother laughed. "You? In a house like that?"

He stilled, though he knew she didn't mean anything hurtful by the comment. "Would that be so ridiculous, me wanting and having a home?"

She laughed again and patted his arm. "We Adamses weren't meant to be tied down by such mundane chores as taking care of a house."

He knew that philosophy well, he'd grown up on it. Still, something deep within him yearned for things to be different.

"Besides," his mother continued with raised eyebrows, "if you were meant to have a place like that, neither Sally nor Darlene would have left you standing at the altar."

"Nice, Mother."

"Look, darling, we all know you're not cut out for that kind of life. Mowing lawns, chasing children . . . watching football."

She had no idea what kind of life he was cut out for, she'd never known, but he didn't feel like reminding her of that. Especially when, as he handed her a check, his secretary popped her head into his office.

"Everyone's here, Dr. Adams—oh, hello, Mrs. Adams." Heidi, his usually reserved secretary, stopped in her hurried tracks and flashed a smile.

"Thanks—" Hunter started to say, then ended on a silent moan when six members of his staff crowded into the office behind her. Every one of their conservative tongues waggled at the sight of his mother, looking twenty years younger than her fifty-three years, and casually stretching her mile-long legs.

It took him twenty minutes after she left to calm them down enough to conduct his crucial meeting, and another twenty to finish answering the deluge of questions about his mother and her television career.

To top off his irritation, he returned home only to find his wanderlust-driven father sprawled on his bed, booted feet on the spread, and food and drink scattered around the previously spotless room.

"I thought you were in Paris," Hunter said wearily, wondering why his parents couldn't be grown-up as he imagined other parents were. He didn't bother to ask how his father had gotten in. Where there was a chance, Patrick O'Reilly Adams could find a way.

"I was." His father stretched lazily. "All that money you make and you live in this hotel. Well, at least it's got class." He glanced around at the tasteful and expensive decor.

Hunter tipped his head back and studied the ornate ceiling, wondering what he had done to deserve having to deal with both parents in one day.

"Eloise has been busy, I understand," his father said casually.

"She's dead," Hunter said flatly, smelling need, greed, and a whole host of things that aggravated the hell out of him.

"Yeah. But she left you quite a package."

The package that made up one Trisha Malloy filled Hunter's head—soft brown eyes, flowing brown hair . . . and black vinyl.

"What are you going to do with it?"

"Funny . . . your ex-wife asked me the same thing today."

"Your mother? . . . Your mother came sniffing around? Figures," he said with disgust.

"Guess she beat you to it." Hunter shoved his father's feet off the bed.

"You're going to sell the duplex, of course."

"Maybe."

His father laughed. "No offense, son, but what in the

world would you do with a place like that? You don't want to live there."

Was it such a joke that he had a secret fantasy to do exactly that? The place needed work, certainly, but that was superficial stuff. Beneath the dilapidated exterior was a beautifully structured home with more character than he'd seen in some time. It sat in South Pasadena, an affluent area, only minutes from work. So it was the eyesore of the entire block, but he could fix that. And he could turn it from a duplex into a single-family house with no trouble at all.

"My God," Patrick said, studying his son. "You *do* want to live there." He laughed again.

Hunter bit back his sigh. He had a ton of work to do, plus enough reading to keep him up all night. "Was there something you needed?"

Of course there was.

"Well, now that you mention it . . ." His father stretched again and sighed. "I find myself rather short of funds."

Hunter closed his eyes and started counting silently. It was going to be a long—and expensive—night.

By the time Hunter got back to the duplex the following weekend, the gaping hole in the bathroom ceiling had been repaired and the downstairs living space cleared of dust and dirt, courtesy of his efficient cleaning crew.

The pathetic reproductions, however, remained. Regardless, a shimmer of something he almost didn't recognize went through him—hope. The hardwood floors were a wreck, the painted walls were old and peeling, but somehow the place drew him. Despite its appearance, the house was alive with personality.

It was a home waiting to happen.

A home. A real home such as he'd never had, such as he'd only dreamed about.

"I guess I'll have to get a real peephole now, since you've covered up the one in my floor."

Trisha. Hunter hadn't known what to expect, more vinyl maybe, or leather. He certainly didn't expect to see her standing in the doorway wearing a short, full sundress that revealed a set of lean, toned legs a mile longer than the city limits.

She smiled, parting full red lips. "How am I going to see what's going on down here?"

"You should be thanking me. Another guy might not have bothered to catch you."

Trisha walked into the cluttered living room and laughed, a full-throated, easy laugh that made Hunter think of a clear mountain spring.

"Good point," she said. A hint of white, frothy lace peeked out from the low, snug bodice of her dress, making his mouth dry.

He shifted his weight with uncharacteristic nervousness as she appraised the length of his body with undisguised admiration. "I didn't know you had to be so strong to look at things under a microscope."

"I spend very little time looking under a microscope."

"Hmm. Then what *do* you do?" she asked.

"Lots of things. Fly."

"In space?"

He had to smile at her incredulous tone. "Sometimes."

"You're an astronaut."

He should have been used to the way people were impressed by his occupation. After all, he'd exploited it enough times to fund his research. "I'm also a physicist and a space scientist for Jet Propulsion Laboratories, which works under NASA's direct supervision." He was also a JPL payload specialist and a principal investigator, which meant he was the department head, but listing all his various responsibilities always sounded so overwhelming and pretentious.

"Wow." She smiled at him. "That explains the attitude."

"Attitude?"

Her smile widened at his stiff tone. "Yeah, definitely attitude."

"I don't have—" He broke off when she laughed. *No.* He would not respond to her gibe. Not when it was obvious anything he said would only confirm her opinion about him.

"I guess they train you pretty hard when you go into space, don't they?"

Again, he saw that heavy-lidded, sensuous stare, telling him she was as painfully aware of him as he was of her. He didn't think that was a good thing, since he had no desire to be aware of her in the first place.

"Do you have to work out every day?"

"We do train hard," he acknowledged, "but I've come up with a new addition for that training. Catching screaming females as they fall through the ceiling. The more you catch, the stronger you get."

"You *do* have a sense of humor. Oh, I'm so glad," she said with so much surprise, Hunter actually felt like laughing.

"It came with the doctorate."

Again she laughed, and he found himself smiling

along with her. It wasn't often Hunter had such a casual conversation, even less often that he wanted to. It felt strange.

"I'm glad you can enjoy funny things." She gave him an indecipherable glance. "It might help."

"Help? With what?"

Slowly, she drew her pouty lower lip through her teeth. "Did I tell you I'm a bit . . . clumsy?"

"You didn't have to," he said wryly. "It's obvious."

"Well, then . . . you'll appreciate how I managed to leave my freezer open last night. By accident, of course." She flashed him a full smile. "It sort of defrosted."

"It . . . defrosted?"

"By the time I woke up this morning, the kitchen floor had rotted right through."

He stared at her.

"The good news is," she continued brightly, "I now have a new peephole—right into your kitchen."

He groaned. "You're kidding."

"You don't happen to cook in the nude, do you?"

THREE

"Well, do you?" Trisha wanted to know, her eyes brimming with curiosity. "Cook in the nude?"

The damn woman actually looked hopeful! "No, of course not," Hunter said curtly, picturing the new disaster she'd left for him to deal with. Did chaos follow her everywhere? Of course it did, she was Trisha Malloy, wasn't she?

"Didn't think you did."

Her obvious disappointment had him shaking his head. She was incredible. And he was actually considering . . . No. It would be temporary only. Forget her huge, sad eyes. He'd find a way to break her lease. He'd buy her out if he had to.

"Well, I've got to be off to the shop," Trisha announced.

The mention of her shop brought up mental images of silk and satin, leather, and an entire host of erotic pictures that left him unaccustomedly hot under the collar.

"I imagine you have work to do too," she said. "You know scientists. All work and no play."

She was obviously referring to the stereotype of his kind as cold-blooded and ruthlessly single-minded workaholics. Many were. Hunter had a reputation for being just that; he knew this because he'd carefully cultivated the image.

Yet it wasn't true. He felt, and deeply. Probably deeper than most. Sometimes he could be stubborn, but only when he knew he was right. And as far as being cold, he simply didn't choose to share his emotions with just anyone. He was picky. So picky, he had to admit to himself, that he hadn't found anyone to share things with in some time. But he was cautious by nature. He found being distant the best way to deal with people— particularly females.

All females, that is, except Trisha Malloy.

It was becoming increasingly difficult to keep his distance from her. Suddenly he regretted the image he'd projected to her. "I'm not working today," he said. "Other than here, that is."

She shrugged her shoulders in a way that lifted her dress to alarming heights on her trim thighs.

Hunter forced his gaze up to her face. A flash of deep sorrow, of repressed fear, crossed her face, gone so quickly he couldn't be sure he hadn't imagined it. What in the world was wrong? Whatever it was, had *he* caused it? "I want to clear out this apartment," he said slowly.

"You do?"

"Was there anything in here you wanted?"

She looked around at what had been Eloise's apartment, then sadly shook her head. "No, thank you, but . . . no."

She wanted to say something else, he was sure of it, yet she'd changed her mind. "You sure?"

Turning, she made her way to the door. "Sure enough. You renting this apartment out?"

He hesitated. Tension emanated from her in waves. He hated the brief flash of need he glimpsed in her eyes, hated the sympathy that rose within him.

"I'm not breaking my lease, you know." She seemed suddenly small, vulnerable.

"So you've said."

"You're stuck with me."

"I'm beginning to realize that." Having seen her place, he was sure she would leave for the right price, but didn't mention that. He couldn't bring himself to hurt her pride. Hunter understood pride well.

Shrugging as if it didn't matter, when he could see so clearly it did, she said with false cheer, "Well, I've got to go." But she stood there, clinging to the doorknob. "You know, I didn't expect to see you again."

"Did you think I was going to just disappear?"

"One could hope," she murmured. She bent, hiding her face as she petted Duff, who'd just strutted into the room.

"Trisha—"

She turned away, ignoring him.

He bit back the urge to start counting, knowing she'd get a real kick out of that. "I can't just vanish. I'm responsible for what happens here."

She scooped the cat close. "This isn't your kind of place."

"Why do you say that?"

She lifted a dark brow. "I saw your face last time you were here, Dr. Adams, you can't deny that you were . . . disgusted."

"Hunter. And it wasn't disgust."

Her red lips curved as she smiled in polite disbelief. He could remember the slippery feel of her in his arms, remember the startling realization that she'd caught him with his fly open. Could remember, too, how he'd felt touching her new shipment of silk, and picturing her in it. Oh, yes, he'd felt many things that day, but disgust hadn't been one of them.

"Dr. Adams—"

"Hunter," he repeated.

Her eyes sparkled. "So casual," she said. "And we've seen each other only three times."

She was laughing at him. He couldn't remember the last time that had happened. Okay, he could. But he was no longer gawky, skinny, too tall, and twelve. "Not all scientists are stuffy, you know."

"Really."

Her eyes dared him and he couldn't resist. "Really."

"When was the last time you went line dancing?" she asked. "Or got a body part pierced?"

He felt the color drain from his face, and she laughed.

"You're turning green, Hunter."

"Body piercing doesn't appeal to me," he said in a chilly voice that would have had his associates backing off in fear for their lives.

Not Trisha.

"Hmm." She pursed her lips thoughtfully. "Bought any CDs lately? Or traveled—just for the heck of it?"

"Just last week I went to China," he said triumphantly.

She shook her head and set down the black cat. "I saw that on the news. You went to promote international support for your program. And to solicit funds, which definitely doesn't count."

"Why not?"

"I meant traveling for pleasure. *Pleasure*," she said again, slowly, making the word roll off her tongue in a sinful way that had his stomach clenching. "What do you do for pleasure?"

He could tell her what he wanted to do.

"Okay, tell me this. How many pairs of jeans do you own?"

The question threw him. "What?"

She laughed and shook her head. "Never mind. Even if you do have a pair, you probably have them starched and ironed." She sobered. "What's going to happen?"

The bubbly, cheerful woman had him so completely flustered with the quick conversation changes, he could hardly keep up. Then there was the way she kept moistening her lips with little darts of her tongue, even as she let out those verbal shots he thought might be meant as insults. "What's going to happen with what?"

One corner of her red mouth quirked. "You're definitely not a rocket scientist, are you?"

That comment, he decided, was most positively meant as an insult, and he straightened, frowning.

"I don't want to leave this place."

"I know." Though he had decided right then and there, with the sunlight pouring in the huge windows, with the wonderful, if a little scuffed, hardwood floor beneath his feet, that he didn't want to leave either.

He wanted to live here.

He just didn't want a wild *female* neighbor above him—he didn't want a wild female anywhere near him—but until he figured a way to break the lease without hurting Trisha, he'd have to make do.

"My lease—"

"I know," he said with a sigh. "You're not breaking your lease."

"And neither are you." Trisha tried with everything she had to hold back the hurt, yet she knew by the flicker of understanding in his gaze that he'd seen it. But she didn't want compassion, she wanted permanence. "Why are you clearing out this apartment?"

"Well . . ." He walked across the room, ran a finger over a particularly gaudy high-backed green sofa embroidered with red roses, making her smile when he shivered with distaste.

But her amusement faded instantly at his next words. "I'm thinking of moving in."

"Moving in," she repeated stupidly.

"You sound thrilled," he noted wryly.

Thrilled? It was her worst nightmare. Her landlord would practically live with her, and he was self-righteous, unbending, stubborn . . . gorgeous.

Oh, get ahold of yourself, she thought furiously. Having Dr. Adams live below her would be like having Aunt Hilda and Uncle Victor back in charge of her life, no matter what her hormones believed.

"You could leave," he suggested with great expectation.

"Never."

His eyebrows rose at her vehemence, but he said nothing.

"I'm not leaving," she said again firmly.

He just looked at her.

So he was one of those people who used silence as a weapon. She hated that. "I'm *not* leaving," she said again, firmly. "I'm staying. *Forever.*" His words surprised her.

"Don't you think we'd make good neighbors?" he asked.

His eyes mocked her, dared her to protest. But Trisha had adopted a new policy in her life, and she refused to be cowed by anyone. "I think we'd make rotten neighbors."

His gaze remained directly on her, his hands in his pockets, but she could feel the inexplicable sensual tug between them as if they had been wrapped around each other.

She wasn't sure it was an entirely bad feeling, which annoyed her into baiting him. "I won't change my lifestyle."

Though he didn't crack a smile, he was definitely amused. She could see it in the line of his straight shoulders, in his easy stance, in his shining green eyes. "You mean you'll continue to peek through holes at me while I'm in the bathroom? You'll crank your music until the windows shake? You'll manage to destroy every floor in your apartment? Or . . ." And now his gaze did dip, ran with leisure over the peekaboo lace camisole revealed by her scoop neckline. His amusement vanished and the heat of his gaze scorched her skin. His voice seemed husky, thick. "You'll continue to model your stock on a regular basis?"

"All of the above," she assured him softly, only marginally satisfied to see that his breathing was as uneven as hers. *This is crazy. We don't even like each other, and we're hopelessly attracted.*

"Well, then," he said in a soft voice. In a move that surprised her, he reached out and playfully tugged a strand of her hair. "I guess we're in for an interesting time of it, aren't we?"

◆━━━━━◆

They *were* in for an interesting time, no doubt about it. In fact, Trisha thought about little else as she drove into work the following morning. And as she told her story, to her assistant and dearest friend in the world, she couldn't help but wonder what would come of it.

"He's *moving in*?" Celia's mouth fell open, revealing the pierced stud in her tongue. "The spacey scientist is moving in below you?"

"He's not a spacey scientist, Celia," Trisha said, feeling a twinge of guilt as she replaced a stack of thigh-high stockings on the shelf. After all, hadn't she called him that very thing before she'd met him? "He's a *space* scientist. And his name is Hunter," she added primly, sorry she'd given him the unfair nickname.

Celia laughed and her jet-black spiked hair shook while the row of silver cuffed earrings lining her earlobe jangled. "Hell of a name for an old, stuffy, scrawny guy with spectacles."

"Uh . . . he doesn't wear spectacles." No, Hunter's green gaze had been sharp as a tack. And he'd been the furthest thing from scrawny she'd ever seen. "He's not old either." She set a sapphire silk push-up bra on a shelf, then yanked at her own scooped neckline, happy with her lace camisole, unhappy with how much of it showed out of her sundress.

"Not there," Celia said, moving the bra over on the shelf so that it complemented the matching swatch of panties. "There. So he's not old and he doesn't wear glasses. What does the spacey—er, *space* scientist do? Measure molecules?"

Trisha pictured the undeniably sexy Hunter Adams hunched over a microscope. "Maybe."

"So, are there going to be *rules* where you live now? No music after nine o'clock and stuff? Good Lord, Trish, after what your God-fearing aunt Hilda did to you in the name of religion, I'd have thought you'd run screaming from another authority figure. *Wait!*" Celia pried a red satin teddy from Trisha's crushing grip. "Now I know you're upset. You're mutilating the goods."

"I'm not upset." A big, fat lie. She hadn't lied to her friend since the third grade, when Aunt Hilda had prohibited her niece from playing with Celia simply because Celia's father was from Puerto Rico and unemployed.

"You're lying to me," Celia said with certainty, worry filling her dark eyes. Hastily, in the interest of damage control, she reached for the rest of the stock in front of Trisha. "I had a dream about this."

Trisha rolled her eyes.

"No, I swear. There was this little mouse, and she had this great big mean aunt mouse who—" She broke off at Trisha's long look. "Well, I did."

"You've been reading that dream-interpretation book again, by that New Age guru Dr. What's-his-name, haven't you?"

"So?"

"Honey, you have *way* too much time on your hands."

"Tell me what's the matter," Celia said stubbornly, uninsulted.

"Nothing." Trisha let Celia take over displaying the stock. How could she concentrate on silky underthings when at this very moment, her new neighbor—and the bane of her existence—was moving in? *Rules?* The very thought had her insides tightening uncomfortably. She'd had enough rules to last her a lifetime. "No rules," she vowed, not realizing she spoke out loud.

"Right." Celia smirked. "Landlords always have rules. And now you're going to live with yours."

"I'm not living *with* him, just above him. And I'm a grown-up. I'll do what I want." A little sliver of doubt crept up her spine. Too many years under unrelentingly strict authority, she thought miserably. It wouldn't start again, it wouldn't.

"It's not an easy thing," Celia commented, watching her carefully. "Doing what you want. Not when you've never been allowed to."

"I'm doing fine."

"Yeah. Now that Hilda's dead and buried." Her voice was soft and kind, and so was the hand she laid on Trisha's arm. "I'm proud of you Trish, real proud. You've created a life for yourself, and you deserve that more than anyone I know. But as much as you pretend to be wild and free, just below the surface lives that repressed, frightened girl you used to be."

"I'm not repressed and frightened," Trisha protested, self-consciously yanking down the upward-creeping hem of her dress. "Look," she said, gesturing to the lace peeking out her cleavage. "Does this look like a woman who's repressed?"

Celia laughed, her eyes warm. "Sweetie, I *know* you. You're constantly checking to make sure you're not showing too much. Didn't you just return that fabulous leopard shipment because it seemed too daring for the shop? Face it," she said gently. "It's not easy for you to let go."

"I'm selling lingerie, aren't I?"

"Yes, and you're doing a wonderful job. But you're still not comfortable with it. That's okay, it'll come. But let this landlord thing slide off your back. Don't let him get to you. There's always another place."

"No!" Trisha took a deep breath and forced herself not to yank up the bodice of her dress. She'd moved eighteen times in eighteen years and had promised herself never to do it again. She loved her place, and Eloise had wanted her to have it.

She *wouldn't* move. "I just want to be free to do what I want. That's all. It's not asking too much, I know that."

"Well, you've done what you want here," Celia said, glancing around the shop. There were at least eight people milling around the small place and it was only noon. "We're keeping our heads above water. Most businesses fail in their first year, but not this one. Thank God, since we've both grown fond of eating. Some of us more than others, of course," she added with a grimace at Trisha's lean, petite figure, then down at her own slightly too curvaceous one.

With a sense of satisfaction Trisha looked around the shop. Organized chaos reigned. Leather and Lace was located in the very favorable area of Old Town Pasadena, where locals and tourists alike walked the quaintly gentrified streets night and day. As a result, she was almost always busy. Her clientele ran the gamut from businessmen to college students, and all their trade was equally important to Trisha. She loved this shop with a passion that didn't surprise her, since the place signified her first taste of freedom.

"I almost forgot," Celia said, biting her lip, looking uneasy. "Your uncle Victor called. Said he missed you at home over the weekend."

Just the name unleashed a flood of miserable memories along with feelings of overwhelming guilt, self-doubt, and low self-esteem. She tugged at her dress again. "I'll call him back later."

"He said you wouldn't." Celia shrugged. "Hey, don't give me that trapped-doe look. I avoid my parents when they call too." She gave Trisha a smacking kiss on the cheek, squeezed her hand, and moved toward a group of tourists. "Good day, ladies. Yes, that's genuine silk. And let me tell you, it's heavenly on bare skin. . . ."

Throat tight, Trisha turned away, thankful to have the best friend anyone could ever have. Making her way through the store, she opened the back room, which doubled as a closet and her office. She just needed a minute to relax, and she'd be fine. Inhaling deeply, she closed her eyes.

"Imagine that I actually thought you were kidding about destroying the floor in your kitchen."

She jolted at the deep, unbearably seductive voice. Heart hammering, she turned to face the man who had knocked her world off its axis.

Dr. Hunter Adams filled the doorway, watching her quietly.

"It's a sin to have a voice like that," she said without thinking, tucking her hands under her folded arms to keep them from yanking at her hem.

"A sin?" He cocked his head questioningly.

His voice could melt the North Pole, but she didn't see any reason to stroke his ego. Not when he stood there looking at her with an intense, inscrutable gaze. "Never mind."

"Your shop is . . . something."

She tried not to care about what he really thought of her shop and what she did for a living, but at this moment she didn't feel strong enough to defend herself. "Yes, it's something."

"Have you always done this?"

"You mean sell panties?" She imagined Aunt Hilda rolling over in her grave, and let out a little laugh. "No. But I've always wanted to do something unusual."

"Well, congratulations; you succeeded."

Her amusement drained. "I'm sure you didn't drive all the way over here to insult me."

He raised his eyebrows. "I didn't insult you."

Not with words. "You've made no secret of what you think of me and what I do."

"You have no idea what I think of you," he murmured. "You seem upset," he continued in the slow, careful manner that made her think of a man who was stuck in a canoe without a paddle, an image that for some reason made her want to giggle. "Is something the matter?"

Yeah. He was driving her crazy. "No."

"Hmm. You're a horrible liar, Trisha. It's the eyes; they give you away."

She sighed. So much for her moment of peace and quiet. "How did you find me?"

"I saw you come in here. What's the matter?"

"I said, nothing."

His eyes narrowed, and in the tiny space not taken up by her files and the desk, she managed to turn from him. He wasn't going to let it go, and his probing eyes seemed to see far more than she was willing to explain. If only he'd let her alone for a few more minutes, she could have gotten herself under control. Inhaling deeply, she forced herself to relax her shoulders and drop arms to her sides. Yeah, the cleavage of her dress slipped and the hem hiked up, but that was what they were supposed to do.

"Trisha. Talk to me."

Distraction, she decided. He needed to be distracted. "What was that about the floor in my kitchen?" she asked over her shoulder.

Resignation flitted across his features. "My kitchen now has a sort of skylight into yours."

Again, the urge to giggle shocked her. "I'm sorry."

"Hmmph."

Control, she reminded herself. *Confidence.* Not easy under the best of circumstances. Next to impossible with this man standing so close to her. "Handy thing, a skylight," she ventured.

"Not much privacy." He looked piqued. "I *like* privacy."

So did she. After enduring years of surprise room searches, it meant everything to her. "Maybe it's overrated." Now he glowered and she nearly laughed at how easily she could rile him. "I really am sorry," she said kindly. "Did you come down here to buy some . . . underwear?"

"No." He seemed to speak through his teeth. "Not from here."

"I stock some beautiful things," she pointed out, enjoying his obvious discomfort with the subject. It seemed sort of incongruous, this big, gorgeous man looking so prim and proper. Unless . . . Oh dear. "Is there a . . . wife?" She held her breath, strangely relieved when he shook his head. Beneath his casual denial she sensed pain, and she knew she had to stop pushing him, but her insatiable curiosity got the better of her. "Girlfriend?"

"I didn't come to buy underwear, for me or anyone else," he assured her grimly, taking a step into the only available space left in the entire room—directly in front of her.

No wife, no girlfriend. The knowledge shouldn't have sent a thrill through her.

"If you don't want underwear, how about a bathrobe?"

"No, thank you." He took another step. Their toes touched.

"Nightwear?" she squeaked.

"I don't wear any."

"Oh, my," she whispered.

He filled the office with a sort of devastating male grace, watching her with an unmistakable light of awareness in his eyes. He studied her slowly, from her low neckline, to her short hemline, and everywhere in between.

Suddenly the stuffy scientist didn't seem so stuffy, but the room sure did. "What *did* you come for?" she asked, her voice low and quavering.

His jaw tightened, and he took a deep breath, which brought him within a fraction of an inch from Trisha, who suddenly couldn't breathe. Slowly, she tipped back her head and looked at him, swallowing hard at his intense expression.

"Hunter?"

"Hmm?"

"Why are you here?"

A wordless sound of frustrated humor escaped from him. "I haven't the foggiest." His big hands touched her shoulders. "For some ridiculous reason, looking at you made me forget."

"You forgot? That's ridiculous—"

But the words were swallowed by his mouth.

FOUR

Before Trisha could draw a startled breath, Hunter had gathered her close to him and gently slanted his mouth over hers. Despite her "seize the day" philosophy, she'd kissed only a few times before. But even with her inexperience, she knew Hunter was no ordinary kisser. She could feel the strength in his arms, the immense power in his body, and how he held it all in check. The challenge was there, certainly, so was the provocation, but all without the demand she'd have expected, and she trembled at the onslaught of surprising, gut-wrenching passion. Inhaling the warm, male scent of him, she opened her mouth to his, gripped his shirt, and held on.

Deepening the kiss, Hunter pulled her even closer, making her sigh in delight as she felt herself molding to every inch of his fully aroused body. Instinctively, her hips pressed against his, making him groan softly. Excitement and a delicious shiver traveled up her spine, followed by his hands.

"Shut the door," he murmured into her mouth,

turning them both when she did, nudging her up against the wood.

Trisha, dizzy with a swirling hunger she'd never before experienced, grabbed his shoulders for support as her world spun wildly.

Trailing his lips over her jaw, he whispered hoarsely, "God, Trisha, what are you doing to me?"

She didn't know, but if it was making his knees half as weak as hers, she could sympathize. But then he nibbled at her ear and she couldn't think at all. Nothing, *nothing*, had ever felt so good.

Leaning over her, his hands caging her head against the smooth wood of the door, Hunter kissed her throat, then the drumming pulse at the base of her neck.

No longer certain she could stand, Trisha dropped her head back. It hit the door with a thunk. "Hunter," she managed.

Luckily, he understood the single-word plea, for he brought his arms around her, gently thrusting his thigh between hers. The material of his pants rubbed against the bare skin of her legs. "Oh, my," she gasped, and he did it again. "Oh, my goodness."

"So profound," he whispered, laughter and more than a little awe in his voice.

"It's just that I had no idea. . . ."

"Me, either." His mouth came back to hers, hot and hungry. Her dress inched up as his muscled thigh eased her legs farther apart.

She was quivering, hot and cold at the same time. This had never happened to her, and she couldn't quite believe it was happening now. The crazy impulse to beg him to make love to her right here, standing up against the door, nearly overpowered her. The pure recklessness of the thought startled her so, she surfaced slightly from the mist of arousal.

So many years of being controlled, browbeaten, and too shy and unconfident were washed away in an instant. "Hunter, I don't understand this." But she pulled his mouth back to hers.

The door slammed open, smacking Trisha in the rump and propelling her full force into Hunter. He grabbed her easily, regaining their balance with an almost feline grace.

"Trish, I—" Celia's voice seemed loud in the stunned silence of the room.

Trisha dropped her forehead to Hunter's chest, wondering if she could possibly be lucky enough to have a huge hole swallow her up.

"Oh. Oops," Celia said.

Embarrassed, Trisha backed slowly out of Hunter's embrace and turned to face her friend.

"The space scientist, I presume," Celia said dryly, her eyes burning with avid curiosity as she studied Hunter. "Conducting a new experiment? Never mind"—she raised her hand—"don't answer that. I'm gone. In fact, I was never even here. Never saw ya." With a wide grin, she backed out of the room and shut the door.

For once, words failed Trisha.

Hunter had his hands on his hips. His brow was creased, his face dark with a moody concentration she didn't know if she wanted to understand. But his eyes still held the fire of barely leashed passion.

"Do you have any idea what the hell just happened between us?" he demanded.

She smiled weakly. "Absolutely none."

He nodded thoughtfully. "Pretty intense."

"You could say that again," she muttered, running her hands over her hips to smooth down her dress.

His gaze followed her movement. He looked about as far removed from a stuffy scientist as he could get, and none too thrilled about it. "That's some dress, Trisha."

Used to criticism, she automatically stiffened, just managing to bite back the surge of defensiveness. "Isn't it?"

"I'm sure I didn't mean that the way you seem to have taken it."

"Forget it."

"Trisha."

"Just forget it."

"No, wait a minute. Tell me you're going to give me more credit than thinking I would actually criticize your clothes."

She didn't want to hear him lie, not when he'd made it so obvious what he'd thought of her. *Yeah, but that was before they'd kissed with wild abandon.* Dammit, this was out of control. "Maybe we should back up a bit," she suggested.

"Back up," he repeated. "To that kiss?"

"No." She had to take a deep breath. "To why you're here."

"Oh." His face tightened into a scowl. "I wanted to talk to you about your kitchen floor—or my ceiling—depending, of course, on which apartment you're standing in."

Oh, yeah. She'd nearly forgotten that not only had she made quite a first impression by falling through his bathroom, she'd also nearly destroyed his kitchen. "I'm sorry."

"You've already said that," he pointed out smoothly. "I don't expect you to keep saying it."

He had no way of knowing that it was a terrible habit of hers, drilled into her during childhood. Apologizing profusely, then continuing to do so, had become a life-long habit. A self-destructive habit she had promised herself she would break.

"I don't have a key to your apartment," he said, still watching her carefully. "And I need to see the full extent of the damage."

Reaching into her desk, she pulled her purse from the bottom drawer, took her front-door key off the ring.

"Thank you."

"I'll reimburse you for the damage, of course." *With what?* She had a stack of bills a foot high in the upper right drawer, awaiting attention.

"It won't be necessary. I'm planning on doing some renovations while we're at it."

His warm, work-roughened fingers brushed against hers as he reached for the key. She glanced up at him to find him studying her with now-familiar intensity. Something strange unfurled within her. *Longing*, she realized with some surprise, and it annoyed her. "I caused the damage," she said stiffly. "I'll pay for it."

"There's insurance."

"There's also a deductible."

He sighed, dropped his gaze down to their fingers, still entwined around the key, and studied them silently. "We seem to have gotten off on the wrong foot here, Trisha."

"No doubt."

"The kiss might have made it worse."

"Probably."

He lifted his head. "I'm not going to apologize for it, since I don't seem to regret it."

"I see." She told herself she couldn't think of one reason why her heart took off galloping again.

"We're . . . different, Trisha."

She smiled. "That's quite an astute observation, Dr. Adams."

He didn't return the smile. "Maybe we could transcend some of those differences."

"I doubt it," she said quite truthfully. He wasn't likely to loosen up and she certainly wasn't about to lace up, not ever again.

"We could always kiss again," he suggested.

"Kissing won't convince me to break the lease."

His other hand came up, sandwiching her hands between his large, warm ones. "That kiss had nothing to do with your lease."

"What *did* it have to do with?"

"I have no idea," he admitted, dropping her hands and stepping away. The back of his thighs encountered her desk, and he sat.

He looked stunningly right sitting there, his elegant clothes hugging that sleek body. It made her mouth water with the urge to touch him again, to do exactly as he suggested and go for another bone-melting kiss.

But that was impossible. It shouldn't have happened in the first place. "Look," she said. "We kissed. No big deal."

"Right," he echoed, with a slow nod of his head. "No big deal." He folded his hands together and watched her.

"It happens all the time." Not to her, she thought. Never to her.

He looked very unpleased. "Not to me."

"We definitely shouldn't do it again."

"Wouldn't be wise."

"We're *different*, as you say."

"Most certainly different." He spoke with some irony, reminding her of his dry sense of humor.

Hunter glanced at a box on a corner of her desk. Black fishnet stockings spilled over the edge. His jaw hardened, and he swallowed hard, but she couldn't decide if it was disgust or excitement. "Yes," he said slowly. "We're quite different."

"But you're still moving into the duplex."

"Yes," he said. His hands gripped the wood of the desk beneath him, giving him away.

"Hunter?" Uneasiness filled her. And suddenly she knew. "You said something about renovating. Oh, no. *No*," she repeated firmly, trying not to panic. "I'm not moving out so you can turn that place back into a one-family house. I'm not."

Standing, he pocketed the key she'd given him. Regret crossed his face before it was carefully masked. "I also would like to see a copy of your lease, when you get a chance." He moved to the door.

"Why? So you can find a way to break it?" Her voice sounded perfectly even, making her proud. She locked her knees together so he couldn't possibly see them wobble. "There *is* no way to break it. Eloise was careful about that."

"I just want to read it, Trisha," he said evenly, kindly, which was the last straw.

"I'm not leaving," she repeated, crossing her arms. Nor would she ever, *ever* kiss him again, no matter how much her body craved the taste of him.

No way at all.

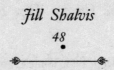
"Just try it. Wear it home. Maybe it'll grow on you," Celia suggested with a wicked gleam in her eyes later that afternoon.

Trisha glanced down at the black, short, snug cotton ribbed dress Celia had designed. "It's . . . tight."

"Is that all you can say?"

Guilt lanced through her. All her life, all Celia had ever wanted was to be a designer. "It's also beautiful."

"Yeah. And you look incredible in it. It shows off your every curve."

Which was exactly what Trisha was afraid of. "I have too many."

"And what a curse *that* is," Celia said with a disgusted laugh. "My designs were made for a body like yours."

Trisha had to admit, it felt terrific to wear something so flattering. She actually felt pretty. "I think I like it," she whispered, stepping into the matching black sandals Celia had brought.

"Good. So maybe I could have some made up?"

"Absolutely," she said, smiling into Celia's hopeful face. "We can sell these."

"Thank you." Celia's eyes were suspiciously bright. "You know how much this means to me."

"Yes. We've been dreaming together for years, Celia. This is the year that they all come true."

"Yeah." Celia nodded thoughtfully. "You were locking lips with the scientist guy today."

Trisha sighed. "Don't tell me how stupid it is. I already know."

Laughter flickered in Celia's expression. "It's only

stupid if the kiss went bad. Which, given my view of the thing, didn't happen."

No, it hadn't been bad, not by a long shot. "It was a bout of temporary insanity. I'm not interested."

"Okay."

"We're too different," she said, echoing Hunter's sentiments.

"Okay."

"And—"

"I said *okay*." Celia interrupted with a laugh. "But methinks the lady doth protest too much."

Celia's last comment gave Trisha pause on her short drive home. *Had* she protested too much? Was there any reason why she couldn't enjoy Hunter *and* her newfound freedom at the same time? Of course not.

But she sensed within him a hesitation that matched her own. He didn't want anything between them any more than she did. Even that fiery kiss they'd shared had made him frown thoughtfully. No, he wouldn't be chasing her anytime soon, though she didn't know why not.

But it was fine with her, just fine.

Turning onto her street, she sighed. She loved this quiet, oak-lined street beyond reason. She pulled into the driveway of the duplex, thinking she also loved this house beyond reason.

Oh, the place needed work, but beneath the shabby exterior lay the strong, beautiful, turn-of-the-century house she wanted to live in forever. Each room had character, and she just couldn't imagine leaving.

Yet she knew without being told, her days at the duplex were limited.

Only if she let them be.

Eloise had made her a promise, and God bless her

soul, Trisha was going to do her best to make sure that promise was kept.

Hunter Adams, if he chose to stay, was stuck with her.

Hunter's salvation, which was and always had been work, would have to wait. Much as he craved the pleasure of researching, drawing up data/theory comparisons, developing his projects, and designing them to fit into his missions, he couldn't very well go off and leave the duplex as it was.

The floor had sagged under the flow of water from Trisha's refrigerator. For all he knew, the damn thing could give and he'd have a gaping hole—again. But at least Trisha had just been kidding about another peephole. He sighed, breathed deeply for patience, and once again gingerly touched the soggy floor with his toe.

The black cat Trisha had called Duff strutted into the kitchen and eyed him. His tail swished, silently suspicious as only a cat can be.

"You see this?" Hunter asked the cat, nodding to the floor. "Do you see what she's done?"

"Mew." Duff sauntered over to his bowl, sniffed delicately, and turned up his nose at the dry food. Coming close, he bent his head and rubbed it over Hunter's ankle.

"Flattery will get you everywhere." He scooped up the cat and stroked its sleek back for a long moment before letting it go.

Then he tested the floor again, concerned. "The woman is a walking disaster," he muttered. "And I have a feeling she's only just begun wreaking havoc on my life."

Duff meowed his agreement and steered clear of the sinking floor.

No doubt about it, the entire thing would cave under too much weight. The linoleum, already old, had peeled back at a seam, and the water from the freezer had seeped deeply into the crack. Beneath, the plywood had rotted. God only knew what lay beneath that, but hopefully some pretty sturdy joists.

He took in the rest of Trisha's clean but amazingly cluttered kitchen. The floor was covered with the same black-and-white-checkered linoleum that he had downstairs, probably from the early fifties. It made his eyes cross to stare at it, especially when juxtaposed with the high-gloss red paint that had been used to disguise the old cabinetry of the kitchen.

Standing between the black refrigerator and the equally black stove, he had a clear view of the rather large room. Above the surprisingly attractive wood dining alcove, the walls were filled with pictures. Not personal photos, he noted with his usual attention to detail, but a collection of paintings, postcards, and drawings that made him wonder about Trisha's private life.

The window frames had been painted red, contrasting with the bright white walls. Across the floor, she'd scattered throw rugs, none identical, but each somehow complementing the others. The counter that separated the cooking area from the living space didn't seem to be available for eating at, not with what were obviously samples of the merchandise she sold covering every spare inch.

On top lay a black leather thong bikini. Irresistibly curious, he picked up the bottom of the thing and stared at the tiny swatch that was expected to cover the essentials. It took him a minute, but he finally figured out that the long black strip of leather was the back. Just looking at it gave him the urge to yank at his own underwear. How did women stand wearing such things?

Beneath the bikini lay a soft, creamy ivory chemise, delicately lined in fine lace—with snaps at the crotch.

His every muscle tightened.

In a rare but fatally stupid move, he'd kissed Trisha Malloy. And she'd kissed him back, with such breath-stopping, sweet-tasting hunger that he got hard just thinking about it. No denying it, a dangerous attraction existed between them, dangerous because he had no intention of acting on it.

A woman was the last thing his life needed, especially a woman so opposite himself as Trisha. He hoped she felt the same way. He didn't want to hurt her, but he knew women tended to think very differently than he did.

Didn't he have two ex-fiancées to prove that?

He had no need for a woman, other than for the obvious, quick diversion, and only then with someone equally uninterested in any sort of permanence. He ran across that sort of woman surprisingly often in the sophisticated circle of acquaintances associated with the lab. Understated, elegant, intelligent, and wealthy in their own right, they often provided entertainment as well as funding for his projects.

Trisha Malloy was not that sort of woman. He'd seen the flash of intelligence in her eyes, but nothing about her was understated or wealthy. And as for elegant . . . he glanced down at the scrap of leather still in his fingers.

The sudden blare of music had him dropping the bikini.

Then came her soft, musical voice, the only voice in his history that could make his insides tighten in anticipation.

"Looking for me?" she wanted to know.

FIVE

Hunter whirled to face Trisha. At the sight of her, his mouth went dry and his greeting croaked out, going unheard over the roar of the music.

Her hair had gone wild in the light wind, the long wavy brown strands flying everywhere. Neatly encased in a body-hugging black dress that showed off her every sensuous curve, she swayed gently to the beat of the music. "How's it going up here?" she asked with a secret little smile.

"I—uh . . ." Oh, great. He'd lost his ability to form a complete sentence. "Fine," he managed.

"Doesn't look like you've done much."

"I had to buy supplies and discuss the problem with a contractor."

"When does he start?"

"Who?" He just wouldn't look at her; that should keep his brain functioning.

"The contractor," she said patiently. "When will he get here?"

"*I'm* going to fix this floor."

"*You?*"

She looked annoyingly incredulous. "It's just a matter of following procedures."

"Which, I imagine, you're good at."

Another jab, but this one offered with a sweet little smile that addled his brain. "I can do this," he said more stiffly than he intended.

"Hmm."

"What does that mean?" he asked.

"Nothing," she said.

"Tell me."

"Fine. I just didn't think you were going to attempt this by yourself. In fact, I think I'm better suited for this than you."

"You?" He laughed when she nodded her head. "No way."

"Why not?"

"Because you're a walking disaster area!" He crossed his arms in a gesture he recognized as ridiculously childish. Dropping them purposely, he said with forced calm, "I'm *not* going to let you handle the construction here."

"Why? Because I'm female? Or because I don't have a Ph.D.?"

"Neither," Hunter said, taking note of the sudden coolness in her tone.

"Why, then?"

"Because you have a habit of creating chaos in everything you do."

She ignored him and danced into the kitchen.

Her perfectly showcased rear continued to rock to the beat of the music as she surveyed the mess her refrigerator had made of the floor. Hunter slammed his hands into his pockets and studied the ceiling.

He would not, no matter what, kiss her mouth again.

It would be the death of him. She represented everything he couldn't deal with; lack of control, recklessness, frivolous behavior—he wouldn't be able to take it.

If only her eyes, and the intelligence he caught behind them, didn't draw him so. "Trisha."

"Can't hear you," she sang out, still refusing to look at him.

He spun her around gently, then backed her to the counter, bracketing her hips. Beneath his hands, he felt nothing but warm, soft woman, which made concentration difficult, but he had to get his point across. "For the record, I never said anything about you not having a Ph.D. That doesn't matter to me." Unable to help himself, he pulled her flush against him just to feel more of her, telling himself he had to hold her to keep her still.

Her sigh just about undid him. "So it's because I'm a woman?"

He dipped his head to her neck, dragging his open mouth lightly down her throat and over her shoulder, taking her weight when her knees buckled. "I never said that either." Lord, she felt good, so right in his arms. Her hands ran over his skin so gently, he nearly moaned at the contact.

For that interminable moment he forgot to resist her, forgot he didn't want this. Then she lifted her head and looked at him, really looked at him, as if she could see into the farthest recesses of his mind.

With a perceptiveness that shocked him, she said quietly, "I want you and I know you want me. What makes this wrong is the fact that you don't *want* to want me."

Hunter went still, but didn't break eye contact. He couldn't because he was inexplicably drawn by the de-

spair he saw reflected in her gaze. Without thinking, he
tightened his grip on her, wanting to comfort.

"You can't break my lease," she whispered, pushing out from between him and the counter. "I won't
leave."

"Did I say anything about your lease?"

"You didn't have to."

"Let's get the floor fixed first," he suggested.

He was patronizing her, putting her off, and nothing
could have infuriated her more. She straightened, pride
nearly choking her. "I told you, I can fix this floor. And
since I ruined it—"

"Fine. We'll *both* fix it," he said, eyebrows creased as
if deep in thought. "I'll need more than two hands."

Trisha crossed her arms and glared at him, trying to
forget the feel of his chest beneath her fingers, the
warm, resilient skin that covered surprisingly tough
muscle. "How condescending of you! First you insinuate
that I couldn't possibly do the job, now you're saying
you'll allow me to *help* you?"

He grimaced and rubbed his chin thoughtfully.
"Ouch. Did I say all that?"

"Yes!"

He sighed. "All right. We'll work as equals. Does
that work for you?"

"Yes. Fine."

"Fine," he repeated. "We'll start tomorrow."

"Because you say so?"

"Because," he said, his patience clearly gone, "it's
too late to start tonight. Do you think you can manage
to keep all the other floors in the place intact until
then?"

Trisha opened her mouth to retort, then realized that

they'd been practically shouting to hear each other over the music.

She moved into the living room and flicked at the volume control just as Hunter followed her, yelling, "And when we do fix it, we'll do it my way or—"

As his voice echoed loudly into the now-silent living room, he blinked in surprise. Trisha laughed at the discomfort on his face. "We'll do it your way or what?"

"Or . . . Oh, hell." His glance was wry, self-deprecating. "You drive me crazy."

"I'm beginning to see that," she noted dryly, hiding the sting his words caused. This was what she'd fought to win her freedom for? To be stuck with a neighbor who reminded her daily of her failings? No, thank you. Right then and there she'd have called him prim and proper, just for the pleasure of riling him again, except for one little thing.

No one prim and proper could possibly kiss with as much talent as Dr. Hunter Adams possessed. "Does everything have to be your way, Dr. Adams?"

Frowning, he crossed his arms. "You like to be contrary."

"Yeah, I do." It was a wonderful defense, as was sarcasm. It usually held most people sufficiently at bay, but not this man. "Just like you like to be in control."

He raked his fingers through his blond military-cut hair, looking frustrated. The way it stuck up only made him more attractive. "Control is a good thing," he told her grimly, as if he were trying to convince himself. He moved to the door. "A very good thing."

As he started to shut it behind him she smiled wickedly and called out, "If you're going to cook breakfast in the nude tomorrow, will you knock on the walls so I don't miss it?"

His shoulders went tense, and his face, just before the door covered it, was entertainingly dark.

She waited for the slam of the wood.

But he cheated her, shutting it very quietly.

Trisha saved Sundays to rejuvenate herself. After six fast-paced days, she needed peace. Oh, she loved the shop, wouldn't consider giving it up. But the worries and stress that came with running her own business never faded.

To please herself, she never rose before ten o'clock. This was mostly a reaction to the way her aunt Hilda had made her rise at the crack of dawn to go to mass and pray for her "wild" soul.

So when a knock came at her door at six A.M., Trisha merely groaned, flopped over, and covered her head with a pillow.

No way would she get up. That delivery—or whatever it was—would simply have to wait. Or better yet, go away.

"Come on, sleepyhead, you've got a floor to repair with me this morning."

No. It couldn't be. Her brain was just playing some sick sort of joke on her.

"I even brought you coffee as a peace offering."

Good Lord, it was. She would recognize that voice anywhere, even before sunrise on a Sunday morning. She swore—quite unladylike.

He made a sound that passed for a laugh, assuring her it wasn't a nightmare. Not him, not this morning, she thought. Not when she felt too groggy to deal with him properly. "Go away," she said succinctly.

"Can't do that." The bed sank at her hip. The heat from his body warmed hers. "You promised to help me."

Trisha burrowed deeper and wished she'd bolted the top lock of her front door. "It's not even daylight yet!"

"This is the best time of the day. I've already run three miles and showered," he claimed with sickening cheer.

He jogged? God save her from frisky scientists. "Bully for you. Go run another three."

"I guess you're not much of a morning person."

"Good guess."

His big hand settled into the middle of her back, jolting her from lazy contentment into sharp awareness. She knew he must have felt her sudden rigidity by the tone of his next words. "What's the matter?" he asked innocently. "Didn't you sleep well?"

No, damn him. His deep green eyes and all the mysteries behind them had haunted her well into the night. She pressed the pillow tighter on her head. "I can't believe you used the key I gave you to come in here like this. I'm changing my locks."

"I like to be in control, remember?"

She offered him a not very polite suggestion about what he could do with that control and where he could take it.

Hunter made a noise that again sounded suspiciously like a laugh. But that couldn't be, she thought from beneath her pillow, because he *never* laughed.

He tugged on the pillow. "Come on, get up. It's not good for the body to lounge around in bed."

In one fluid move, she jerked the pillow off her head and tried to smack him with it, but he easily warded off the blow, grabbed the pillow, and tossed it harmlessly to the floor. Then he grinned at her.

"My body is fine," she grated.

His eyes darkened, and his mouth opened, but whatever he was going to say got smothered with her second pillow to his face.

He grunted at the impact.

"What if I hadn't been alone in this bed?" she demanded.

With great care, he removed the pillow from his face and set it gently on her bed. She had no idea where the question had come from, but given the displeased look on his face, it was far too late to take it back.

What if she hadn't been alone? The very idea was a joke—she was always alone. That's how she wanted it, with only herself to answer to. No rules.

"If you hadn't been alone," Hunter said quietly, his face completely void of expression as he leaned over her, "then I guess I'd have *two* helpers—I mean co-workers—in fixing that floor."

She snorted, sat up, and shoved him off the bed. "Next time, knock."

With a natural agility, he caught his balance and rose. "I'm hoping there isn't a next time."

"Meaning?"

"Meaning if you'd stop destroying this place, I wouldn't have to keep fixing it."

Trisha hated being clumsy. She also hated doing stupid things, but she tended to being the one and doing the other because she often acted without thinking things through. Impulsive, she thought with disgust. And she had yet to learn how to curb her insatiable curiosity. It was what had caused her to fall out of the hole in the bathroom into Hunter's very capable arms in the first place, and it was what had caused her to defrost her refrigerator in the middle of the night because she couldn't sleep and didn't feel like reading.

But as much as she hated her own faults, she hated having them pointed out to her even more. "Maybe you should think twice about moving in downstairs. I could be dangerous to your health."

"No doubt. But you're not that lucky."

"You're taking your chances," she said a little desperately. "I could set the place on fire next."

He ignored her. Silently, he headed to her bedroom door, his body gliding smoothly, easily. Apparently, the man did indeed own a pair of jeans, and they were something. Snug and faded, they fit him like a glove, hugging his lean hips, his powerful thighs, those long legs. So did the T-shirt he wore, the one that revealed the sculpted arms that swung with elegant confidence as he walked.

Not fair, she thought to herself, not fair that a man as annoying as he was could have been given such innate grace, such fluidity of movement.

Where the hell was her stuffy scientist?

More sleep was what she needed, she decided as her body tingled with a yearning she didn't want. Lots more sleep.

"Come on," he said. "Let's go."

She cleared her throat, aware that she'd been staring at him walk away, her mouth open. But she didn't want to get up still in a fog, and risk the chance that she might jump him in her still-sleepy state. "Why don't you start without me," she suggested hopefully, holding the sheet up to her chin.

He gave her a long, thorough look.

Trisha returned the even gaze, refusing even to think about what she must look like sans makeup, her hair rioting around her face.

"Start without you? I already did." Now his lips curved slightly at the edges. "You missed the breakfast peep show."

"You mean . . . ?"

He nodded. "Yep. Made eggs and toast in the buff and you missed it."

She didn't believe him, of course. He was too proper for that. But a nagging sense of doubt held her, as did the dimple of humor tugging at the corner of his mouth. Could he have? That mouthwatering physique moving in all sorts of interesting ways as he worked a frying pan?

"Guess you'll have to find a new hole to watch through," he said casually. "I think I've developed a new habit."

Her mouth dropped open as he shut the door.

It took her hours, *hours* of fetching and holding and generally being useless before Trisha dared to ask her first question of Hunter. "How come you didn't just hire a contractor?"

Plaster dust coated his short hair, but instead of making him look ridiculous and juvenile, the white powder blended like silver hair would have, giving him an elegant air. All the more annoying, because Trisha had no doubts as far as her looks were concerned.

She looked like a wreck.

"I didn't hire one because it wasn't necessary," he said patiently, inspecting the box of easy-set linoleum tiles they'd purchased. "I'm perfectly capable of doing this."

On his knees in the kitchen, with a leather tool belt

slung low on his hips, his T-shirt streaked with flooring compound, he definitely looked capable. But then again, Trisha suspected he would look capable doing just about anything. "Did you really cook eggs in the nude this morning?"

He didn't even blink, nor did he stop what he was doing. "I don't lie, Trisha."

Maybe she *would* have to find a new peephole. "When was the last time you were up in space?"

"Two months ago."

"What did you do up there?" she asked.

He sighed. "You're just full of questions this morning, aren't you?"

She grinned and shrugged. "I have this mean curiosity streak."

"And I wondered how you got yourself into so much trouble." He shook his head.

"Well? What did you do up there?"

He sighed again. "I was the payload specialist for the last space-shuttle mission."

"What was the mission?"

"Mars. Our studies of the Martian analogue samples we obtained led us to some rather critical conclusions concerning meteorological phenomena on that planet."

She stared at him and wondered if he'd spoken in English. "When do you go up again?"

"Maybe next year. I hope."

Trisha thought of how wonderfully exciting his life must be. What a thrill it must give him to be doing important work for the space program. And how dangerous it was. "Do you ever get scared?"

Setting down the box of tiles, he looked at her. His expression was normally intense, focused, whether he was working or just walking, for that matter. But that concentration faded now as he focused on her. "Scared?" he repeated.

"Yeah. As in for your life."

"Sometimes," he said softly. "Being out there can get a little terrifying."

"Being right here on Earth can get a little terrifying too."

"I know."

It unnerved Trisha that the man she thought of as stern and unbending could feel the same emotions she felt, emotions like fear, loneliness . . . need.

Unsettled and needing some distance, she rose from her stiff knees and crossed the floor to the table where she had set their drinks.

Hunter, remaining on his knees in front of the refrigerator, picked up the glue for the tile and began to read the directions. Duff came over to him, sniffing at the can. Without breaking his concentration, Hunter reached out and stroked the cat's back.

Trisha stared at him, watching carefully for any sign that it was all an act. That he couldn't possibly be pleased to be on his knees in her kitchen wasting away a Sunday because of her stupid mistake, that he couldn't possibly enjoy having her cat crawl all over him.

But he wasn't acting, he was just *being*. And it confused the hell out of her. Even when he was speaking to her in the low, dry tone that said he was annoyed—she knew he wasn't really, but just naturally quiet. And the way he looked at her, his eyes all dark and serious and . . . hot. It took her breath away.

So why did he keep up the pretense of wanting his distance? He did have a sense of humor, a great one.

And whether he wanted to admit it or not, he liked being with her.

And dammit, she wanted him to kiss her again. Setting down her drink, she asked, "What does your family think of your profession?"

"They try not to."

"Not to what?"

"They try not to think about me *or* what I do."

She caught a flash of pain rising up from deep within him, but it disappeared so fast she couldn't be sure. He was reading again. "I'd think they'd be proud."

"Think again."

She wasn't getting anywhere along that road. "I bet your job makes you seem attractive to a lot of women."

He kept his gaze on the can of glue, but she could tell by the stiffness of his shoulders, he was no longer trying to read. "Yeah, that's why I took it."

She was getting used to this by now, his dry but deliberately provocative answers. But since she herself was the master of defense by sarcasm, he was out of his league. "So I can expect a lot of traffic coming in and out downstairs?"

Now he dropped his head between his shoulders and studied Duff, who had settled on his legs. "Awfully curious about someone you don't like much, aren't you?" he asked finally.

"I never said I didn't like you," she said cheerfully. But she was going to learn something about this close-mouthed, private man if it killed her. "Why would you move in here when you could probably afford to buy your own place, one that's already fixed up?"

"Are you going to ask me questions all day long?"

"Probably."

He sighed. "You haven't stopped talking since I woke you up this morning."

"Well, *you* woke me up."

"Don't remind me," he said.

"Then you gave me caffeine," she added.

"You'd talk nonstop with or without caffeine."

True enough, but she resented the observation anyway. "I just want to know more about you."

Sighing again, he rolled to his feet with ease. "All right, obviously you're not going to leave me alone until we resolve this. What is it exactly that you want to know?"

Everything. "Why aren't your parents happy about what you do?"

Again, that flash of emotion in his gaze, the one that made her want to hug him. "My parents wanted me to follow in their footsteps."

"Which are?"

"They're creative," he said carefully. "An actress and an artist."

The very opposite of him and his technical kind of intelligence. "So they don't necessarily disapprove, they just don't understand what you do."

"In a nutshell, yes."

It caused him anguish. How well she could sympathize with not being understood. "I'm sorry," she whispered, dazed by this unexpected discovery of common ground. "I would think they'd be very proud of you."

He took a step toward her; Trisha couldn't look away. The music rocked softly. Duff, in the background, meowed for dinner. Down below, on the street, a car honked. None of those sounds registered.

The moment spun out as the intimacy between them

grew, enveloping them in a private cocoon. Hunter took another step, stopping a breath away.

Trisha tipped her head back, her pulse already ragged. In anticipation, her mouth parted.

Hunter leaned close, murmuring her name.

Then her phone rang, and broke the spell.

SIX

Trisha started, then slowly let out the breath she'd been holding.

The phone rang again, and with the noise came reality. Sunday. Oh, dear—Uncle Victor with his weekly dose of guilt and shame.

"Aren't you going to answer it?" Hunter asked, his voice husky.

It did give her some comfort to know he'd been as affected as she. "No."

When the phone rang a fourth time, her palms started to sweat. Dammit, not now, not when she felt so open, so incredibly vulnerable. She wouldn't be able to stand it.

But Uncle Victor missed Aunt Hilda, and didn't just the fact that he called her tell her how much he cared, somewhere deep inside?

Oh, fine. She yanked the receiver off the wall. "Hello?"

"Well, girl, it's about time," Uncle Victor said in the

cantankerous, demanding tone he always used with her. "I've been trying to get you for two weeks now."

"Hello, Uncle Victor." Her stomach already hurt.

"In the name of God, Trisha," he griped. "Turn that blasted noise down."

"I like the music," she pointed out automatically, her every muscle tightening with stress. He couldn't be nice or kind. Never. Not even when he was calling to say he missed his wife, he missed his niece, that he was lonely. "How are you?"

"What?" he bellowed.

"I asked how you were," she repeated dutifully, slightly louder, in deference to the hearing loss that he wouldn't admit to save his life.

"Tough as nails, as always. What the hell have you been doing?"

"I, uh . . ." She glanced at Hunter, who had squatted on the floor and was inspecting their work. He'd obviously forgotten about her. Relieved, she turned her concentration back to the telephone. "Just the usual, Uncle Victor."

"You mean you're still selling that nasty crap to people who have nothing better to do with their time?"

Like the man didn't have a stack of adult magazines dating back twenty years in the woodshed behind the garage. "Selling nasty crap. That about sums it up," she said cheerfully while her stomach clenched. She shot another surreptitious glance over her shoulder.

Hunter didn't even glance up, which relaxed her somewhat. She didn't want him to be an audience to what she knew was coming.

"Good God, girl, your aunt Hilda's probably rolling in her grave," Uncle Victor said roughly, his voice heavy with disapproval. "I'm not sure where we went wrong that you feel you have to do this."

"You didn't go wrong. And it pays the bills." *Sometimes.*

"What's the point, if you can't be proud of what you do?"

"Who said I wasn't proud of what I do?" Dammit, she'd promised herself she wouldn't let him bait her, and here she was, hooked again. From the corner of her eye, she could see that Hunter's stance had stiffened. With all her might, Trisha wished she'd answered the phone in the other room, away from his curious ears.

"Well, you might as well be standing on the street corner, flaunting your wares." Uncle Victor berated her so loudly that Trisha had to pull the phone away from her ear.

Hunter went unnaturally still.

"Standing on the street corner would constitute a different occupation entirely," Trisha observed lightly as the last of her nerves frayed. Hunter shifted suddenly, drawing her attention to his concentrated frown, and she closed her eyes in embarrassment. Oh, well, it wasn't as if she were trying to make a good impression. It was far too late for that.

Besides, she didn't care what he thought of her.

Yeah, and pigs could fly.

"Sassing me!" her uncle said with disgust. "You would never have dared when—"

"Aunt Hilda was alive." She quietly completed Uncle Victor's oft-spoken line.

"I'm just trying to make sure I do what's right by you." Uncle Victor spoke louder than before, a sure sign his temper had been stirred. "I have a duty."

"Your duty has been completed. The fact that I'm rotten to the core—"

Uncle Victor swore colorfully. "Don't you put words in my mouth. I just don't approve of what you do for a living."

"So I've thrown my life away; it isn't your fault," she said dryly.

Hunter rose lithely from the floor. He stepped closer to her, his expression carefully blank. Horrified at what he was hearing, Trisha turned away and struggled to watch her words. She moved as far from him as the phone cord would allow.

The leather of Hunter's tool belt creaked, warning her of his movements as he came close enough for her to feel his body heat seep into her back. "Was there something you wanted, Uncle Victor?" she asked quickly. "I'm really quite busy."

"Just wanted to talk to my niece," he grumbled. "Not like you ever call me."

Guilt lanced through her, which was exactly what he'd intended. Still, she felt like a jerk. "I'm sorry," she said sincerely, dropping her forehead to the wall. "I should call you more often."

"It'd be nice. Instead, you're too busy selling unmentionables to strangers. I can't even tell anyone what you do for a living, girl. Good Lord, if I did, they'd all be beating down your door, thinking you were easy."

A career in the army hadn't softened his manners any. Gruff as they came, and stubborn as a mule once he got a thought into his head. "I'm not easy," she said through clenched teeth.

From behind her, Hunter's big, warm, callused hand settled on her shoulder, making her bite her tongue. Gently but firmly, he turned her to face him, ducking his head to see her face. She stared at his shoulders, fascinated with how the width of them seemed to surround her.

He lifted her chin, the sparks of anger in his eyes startling her. "Hang up," he mouthed.

"Just remember your upbringing, girl," Uncle Victor said in her ear. "Your aunt Hilda and I worked hard to teach you straight."

"Yes, Uncle," she said dully, her heart thumping in response to Hunter's touch, to his nearness. To the empathy he showed. "You did your best."

Hunter reached for the phone, looking determined.

"You can say that again," Uncle Victor said with a snort. "When I think of all we gave up to raise you after your parents died—"

"I know. I'm sorry, I've got to go." But she stood there, locked in miserable memories until she felt a gentle tug on the phone.

Hunter took it from her and set it quietly in its cradle. His expression could no longer be read, but she had no trouble sensing the sudden tension and anger. For some reason, that made her want to cry. "Well, that was fun," she said, striving for humor and falling flat.

He seemed to understand her need to keep things light. "Isn't family something?" he asked quietly, still standing close.

"Oh, my family is something, all right," she said, turning away. It didn't matter what he thought, she told herself. It just didn't matter.

The hand he had left on her shoulder tightened as he gently turned her back to face him. "He was rude to you."

"Isn't that the definition of family?"

"Why do you put up with it?" he asked, his tone suddenly curt, very controlled.

So this was what the space scientist looked like angry. Shakily, she released her breath. He was full of this rage, *for her*. The burst of emotion that realization caused made her legs rubbery. "I guess your family does things different."

"Not much," he muttered. "But I don't let mine get to me."

What he didn't say spoke volumes, and she knew without being told that his family hurt him as much as hers hurt her. "Well, what's family for if not to constantly remind you of every fault and failing?" she quipped.

"It's wrong."

"Doesn't your family ever get the best of you?"

"We're not talking about me." His voice softened. "But family shouldn't hurt."

"No, they shouldn't." Before her eyes, his temper drained. Something flickered in his gaze then. Sympathy? Compassion? Whatever it was, she couldn't handle it, not when the urge to weep still had her eyes stinging. "Let's finish the floor." Again she turned away.

But Hunter just pulled her back. "What do your parents think of good old Uncle Victor?"

"They're gone."

He winced. "Hell. I'm sorry."

"It was a very long time ago. My aunt and uncle raised me, and my aunt died not too long ago, which is why . . . why he calls," she finished lamely.

"Does he call often?"

"Weekly. I usually manage to avoid him, which makes me feel even guiltier."

"Sounds like that's part of his purpose."

"Guilt is his specialty." Why was she telling him this? It would only reinforce what he thought of her. She clamped her jaws shut.

His gaze searched her face deeply, as if he could see past her facade and into her very soul. Uncomfortable, Trisha squirmed away, unwilling to allow this man more insights than she'd already given him.

"I'd probably avoid him too," Hunter observed, setting his hands on his hips. "He didn't have much of value to say about you or your life."

He never did. With a meaningful glance toward the tools, Trisha said, "The floor. I think we should—"

"Is he your only family?"

"Now who's full of questions?"

"Is he?"

She sighed. "Yep. Just good old Uncle Vic and me. The floor, Hunter."

"He sounded . . . demanding."

"He's military," she said with a shrug, wondering at his curiosity. "My aunt wasn't as bad, but she attended mass daily, sometimes more than once. They aren't exactly what you would call openhearted or forgiving."

"Sounds tough. And you were all alone with them, no siblings to deflect some of the anger?"

She never talked about this, not even to Celia. Her new outlook on life—namely, being positive no matter what—didn't allow it.

Diversion was self-defense. Backing away from both him and his touch, she said pointedly, "The floor, Hunter. We've got to finish it today."

Again, he just looked at her, his green eyes seeing far more than she wanted him to. "I'm sorry he upset you, Trisha."

He said this so lightly, with such tenderness and understanding, that her throat tightened again. "I'm . . . just fine."

"Then why are you twisting the phone cord as if you need something to strangle?"

Looking down at her tangled-up fingers in the long cord, she grimaced. "Can we drop this? Please? I'm really rotten with pity."

"I'm not—" He broke off when she walked away from him, heading to where they'd been working. "Gee, I guess we're done talking," he muttered, and followed her.

She knelt, keeping her head down. What was it about this man that stripped her bare? "Are you going to help, or what?"

Yeah, he was going to help. Probably more than he wanted, but dammit if she didn't look unexpectedly small, alone, miserable. God, he was a sucker. Dropping to his knees beside her, he looked into her drawn face. "I'm going to help."

"Good." She sniffed, blew her nose.

His heart broke a little. "For the record, I don't pity you."

"No?" One side of her mouth quirked. "Why not?"

"You're too damned ornery."

She laughed, as he'd hoped she would. Some of her color had come back, he noted, and that relieved him. For one horrified moment, when he'd been pushing her for answers as if she'd been an experiment of his, he'd thought she was going to burst into tears.

It had been a favorite tactic of his mother, and his two ex-fiancées.

Hunter Adams didn't do well with weepy women.

But Trisha, she did something to him, something he was unaccustomed to. Listening to her battle with her uncle for pride and confidence stirred within him a fierce protectiveness he hadn't known he possessed.

It also gave him an insight into the woman who, up until now, he'd looked at only superficially. It shamed him to realize it, but it was the truth.

Trisha Malloy had become far more than just a shell. Beneath the slightly off-center purveyor of fine lingerie lived a surprisingly tough, intelligent, and lovely woman. One, he suddenly realized, he wanted to know better.

Hunter worked days and nights for most of the following week. His current project, only twelve months away from launch, had kicked into high gear. As principal investigator, team leader, and payload specialist, all aspects of the flight would be under his command. The planetary surface lander they were to launch from the shuttle, the one that would study the soil content on Mars, had been ready for some time, but there was still a long list of preparations to carry out, all of which was his responsibility. An exciting task, one he typically thrived on.

But it became difficult to concentrate fully when his new project, the duplex, weighed heavily on his mind. He'd moved his spartan belongings into the lower apartment the weekend before. Now, for the first time in his many years of traveling and hotel living, he needed his own furniture.

He liked that very much, and as he jogged at week's end, he thought over his week.

On Monday, he'd had most of Eloise's furniture picked up by the center he'd donated it to. Now suddenly, or maybe not so suddenly, he'd become eager to dig in and fix the place up.

It was a joke, or it would be if he had told anyone his plans. Dr. Hunter Adams drooling over fixing up a house. But the yearning deep within him, to have a real home that belonged to him, couldn't be denied.

For now he'd start with the lower portion of the house. He told himself he didn't want to take on too much at once, though he knew it was that he couldn't bring himself to fight Trisha for full possession.

He hadn't spent any time with her all week. Which was good, he told himself. It meant she hadn't destroyed or ruined anything. It meant she hadn't caused any trouble. He'd heard her music, and several times he'd heard her laughter.

Halfway through the week, he'd come home at dusk to hear a lawn mower. Curious, since he knew he hadn't paid a gardener, he walked through to the back and suddenly stopped, riveted by a surge of surprise and pure lust.

Trisha, hair piled precariously on top of her head, singing at the top of her lungs and rocking her head back and forth to the tune only she could hear in her headphones, was mowing the lawn. The cropped white T-shirt she wore clung to her damp skin, becoming sheer enough to reveal the outline of her nipples.

His mouth went dry.

Not noticing she had an audience, she moved past him, sashaying her cute little butt, barely covered in the tiniest, shortest cutoffs he'd ever seen.

On her next turn through the yard, she caught sight of him and started in surprise. Stopping, she flipped up the headphones and smiled sweetly—completely unaware of what she'd done to him.

He'd covered the shock of his reaction to her by muttering grumpily and taking over the job of mowing.

That she'd relinquished the chore with only a knowing smile, then disappeared, hadn't improved his mood, or his raging hormones.

The next day he'd come home to find her on the front lawn, giving Duff a bath.

"He rolled on the driveway, under my car," she explained over the yowling feline objections.

"So you decided to punish him by sentencing him to a bath?" he asked, watching in amusement as Duff's ears flattened against his head when she carefully mopped his face.

"He was covered in oil," Trisha explained, leaning back on her knees.

His gaze dipped, and he got an eyeful down her gaping, drenched sundress, enough to render him speechless for a minute. By the time he could speak, words weren't necessary.

Because Trisha, with a wicked smile, threw a soaking wet washcloth in his face. Pulling it away slowly, he glared at her. "What was that for?"

"Take a picture," she suggested with that irritating secret smile. "It lasts longer."

"You're *not* going to provoke me into a water fight."

"No?" Those full lips pouted. "You're no fun."

"So I've been told," he retorted. And, hard as a rock, he'd walked away.

The next morning, while shaving, he'd heard her shower running. Standing there in front of his bathroom sink, staring at himself in the mirror, he'd pictured what she was doing directly above him. He'd gotten hard, again. The image of her wet and soapy had stayed with him for the day, making it necessary for him to spend most of it behind his desk.

He couldn't remember the last time he'd been unable to control his own body, and felt, quite ridiculously, like a teenager.

Now it was Friday, and as his feet pounded the cement, he realized he hadn't seen Trisha the day before, and he wondered what she'd done, if she'd had a good day.

You're no fun.

Trisha's words echoed in his head. No, he *was* no fun, not in her eyes. Which was exactly why he had to stop thinking about her. She was so different, so full of life—happy to live her life as she saw fit, as wildly as she wanted.

He was the complete opposite. Even if he decided to risk it for himself and drown himself in her beauty, they were doomed. He could never make someone like her happy for long.

He had never made *anyone* happy.

As he ran down the dark driveway, past the newly mown lawn, he glanced at his car and came to an abrupt stop.

The scrawled words on his windshield—in what looked suspiciously like lipstick—read:

I'm sorry about the little dent on your fender! Think you could scoot over just a bit more when you park? Keep smiling, Trisha.

Beneath that, she'd drawn a happy face.

Disbelieving, Hunter strode to the back of his car and swore colorfully into the predawn morning. His left bumper had been neatly rearranged, dotted with red paint—the very color of Trisha's ancient Nissan.

He jerked his gaze up and studied the amply wide driveway that ran alongside of his large house. Then he glanced at the equally wide street and the front of the house, where at least three cars could have fitted. *Unbelievable.* A small white, flapping piece of paper had been attached to the fender, catching his eye. With a snort of disgust, he ripped it off, brought it close in the waning dawn and read:

> *Ran out of lipstick! I'm really, really sorry. Hope you have a nice day, Hunter. (This time I insist on paying the damages!) See ya soon.*

A little laugh escaped him. "Unbelievable," he repeated out loud. He spared a last look of disgust at Trisha's offending red car, which didn't appear damaged beyond a few missing flecks of paint. Shaking his head, he shoved the note in his pocket, thankful he'd run, because it looked as though he would definitely need the stress relief today.

Hunter allowed himself one last thought before he focused his energy on his work.

A silent Trisha didn't necessarily mean a quiet one. It looked as if he'd do well to remember that in the future.

Hunter would have liked nothing better than to bury himself in his work, of which he had plenty. He'd been doing it for years. But lately, for some reason he couldn't fathom, his personal life kept interfering.

He'd no sooner set foot in his office when his phone buzzed. His secretary's voice came over the line, sounding surprised.

"You're late."

If he was, it was the first time in his thirty-four years he'd been late for anything. "Seems that way."

"Is anything wrong?"

He smiled grimly. "Lipstick doesn't come off windshields. Remember that if you ever get the urge to paint a guy's window with scarlet lipstick."

"What?" Heidi exclaimed, obviously startled. They'd worked together for nine years and they'd shared exactly three personal conversations—occurring each time Heidi had gotten pregnant and needed leave. "What did you say?"

"Nothing," he answered wryly, shoving a hand through his short hair and sinking into his chair. "What's up?"

"You've got a visitor down at the main building who's awaiting clearance. Sheryl Adams?"

His niece. Tuition time already, he thought with a sigh, and okayed her clearance. Ten minutes later Sheryl entered his office, looking every bit the college student in her opaque black tights, thigh-high black leather boots, and a short black wool jumper over a stark white blouse. Hip-length, straight blond hair bounced as she danced into the room. "Hi, Uncle Hunter!"

Standing, he suffered her jubilant hug and kiss, then extracted himself from her arms when Heidi buzzed him again.

"You've got another visitor at the main desk," she said, sounding wildly curious. Hunter knew two personal visitors to the reclusive Dr. Adams in one day would have Heidi the center of attention at lunch.

Not his mother again, he thought, knowing he didn't have the patience today. Besides, his checkbook couldn't handle it.

"It's a Ms. Trisha Malloy."

Hunter stared at the telephone. *Trisha*. Good Lord, what had she done now that she actually had to seek him out at work? "Send her up," he said wearily, and managed to give a weak smile to his waiting niece.

He'd written Sheryl's tuition check, and had just barely managed to catch her as she flung herself at him in gratitude, when his office door opened.

He heard the soft exclamation of apology.

Hands full of buoyant, happy coed, Hunter jerked his head up to see Trisha turning away.

"Trisha?"

She disappeared around the corner.

Dammit. "Trisha!" Hunter plucked Sheryl's arms from around his neck and strode to his door. "Wait."

Slowly, from halfway down the carpeted hallway, Trisha turned back. The very short, very full skirt of her fuchsia outfit swung wildly around her trim thighs. "I can see you're busy," she said softly, quietly, though her hands fisted at her sides. "I'll just talk to you another time."

He'd never seen her so strangely subdued, so . . . calm and unassuming. Something was wrong, very wrong, and his heart tripped. "Now is fine, Trisha."

But Sheryl, curse her very lovely hide, chose that moment to bounce out of his office, throw her long arms around his neck, and kiss him soundly on the cheek. "I'll never forget this," she vowed cheerfully with a vibrant giggle. "*Never.*"

Without another word, Trisha turned and left.

SEVEN

Trisha forced herself to walk sedately through the NASA complex that housed Jet Propulsion Laboratories. She even managed several halfhearted smiles in response to the few appreciative glances she received.

But once she made it back through the main building and to the parking lot, she started running, her breath catching in her throat, her ridiculous pink pumps slapping dangerously against the asphalt.

What was the matter with her?

She'd come simply to make sure Hunter had gotten her note, to apologize in person. She'd wanted to see if he would accept her offer to get estimates for the damage to his fender so she could pay the bill.

That was absolutely all she'd come for.

It had nothing to do with the fact that she . . . missed him. Nothing at all.

Goodness, she hated liars. And she was lying to herself now. She'd come to see the man who had begun to fascinate her and she damn well knew it.

Just because said man had a tall, leggy blonde hanging all over him meant nothing.

She had no claim on him, nor did she want one. She'd known him for only a couple of weeks, and even then on a casual basis. Their teeny-weeny kiss meant nothing, nothing at all. Dr. Adams could mess around with a dozen such blondes for all she cared.

Right.

That kiss hadn't been teeny-weeny. Nope, it'd been the mother of all kisses, at least in her eyes. Nerves had her fumbling with the lock on her car as her breath huffed out from her run. Her hands were shaking so, that she couldn't fit the key into the lock.

"Trisha."

Hunter's voice came from directly behind her and she nearly leaped out of her skin. Her keys went flying out of her hands.

Hunter squatted down at the same time as she, reaching for the fallen keys, which was how she found herself hunkered down beside her car, staring into his dark green, unfathomable eyes.

Solemnly, he handed her the keys, then slowly pulled her up as he rose. The top of her head came to his chin, she noted with disgust. No wonder he never looked twice at her. The lovely blonde in his office had been nearly six feet tall.

"Why did you run off?" he asked, tugging her gently back when she tried to turn away.

She lifted her chin, assuring herself she couldn't catch her breath from her run, *not* from the way he was looking at her. "You looked pretty busy."

"Did I?" he asked quietly, an annoying smile playing about his lips.

She inhaled deeply at his obvious amusement. "Are you going to deny you had your hands full?"

He laughed, shook his head, then threw his head back and laughed again. Rarely did he let go like this, and Trisha could only stare. When he smiled like that, his entire face lit up, and he became even more handsome, if that was even possible. "I don't see what's so funny," she said haughtily. Freeing her arm from his grasp, she grabbed her keys and hurriedly unlocked her car.

But Hunter laid a hand on the door, deterring her. His eyes still swam with humor, but he sounded sincere when he said, "You came all the way over here, Trisha. It must have been important. Is everything all right?" Suddenly the amusement faded, replaced by worry. "What's the matter? Has something else happened?"

He looked mildly terrified, which helped. Served him right to have a bad moment, and knowing that, she regained some badly needed confidence. How dare he assume that she'd done something else to his precious house. Stubborn as he, she crossed her arms and glared at him.

"Trisha, what have you done now?"

"You mean besides crashing into your car? Or destroying two floors?"

"Yes. Exactly like that."

She laughed shortly. "I can't believe you think I've done something bad."

"Well, have you?"

She just studied her hot-pink fingernails silently, wanting him to suffer.

"Trisha." He put his hands on his hips, the elegantly tailored suit he wore stretching appealingly over his shoulders and back. "Tell me the house is still standing."

She caught it then, the laughter in both his voice and face. The teasing tone went a long way toward soothing her ruffled feathers, but she wasn't finished. "The good news is that the foundation of the duplex is still intact."

She had the immense satisfaction of seeing him lose some color, of watching that wide, chiseled jaw drop open, but she couldn't hold back her laughter.

"Oh, you're funny." He smirked at her. "Are you going to tell me why you came here before I have to attend my meeting? Or are you going to make me sweat all day, wondering?"

So the blonde was still waiting for him. "Wouldn't want to make her wait, now, would we?"

He looked at her blankly, clearly puzzled, for one long moment before he rubbed his chin slowly. If she didn't know him better, she would have sworn he was biting back a smile.

"You think my meeting is with Sheryl," he said finally.

"Is that her name?" Trisha shrugged indifferently. "It could matter less to me." She smoothed down her bright pink jacket, studied her hopelessly scuffed pumps.

"Naturally." But Hunter just continued to stare at her, looking suspiciously pleased with himself.

It was then she realized he had no intention of telling her a damn thing. *Fine.* "I just wanted to know about your car. I want to get estimates done for you so I can pay for the damage."

"Ah, yes, the fender."

"Don't tell me you'd forgotten," she said.

"Did you know that red lipstick is nearly impossible to clean off a window?"

"Sorry." She smiled sweetly, innocently. "But I

didn't know your phone number and you didn't answer my knock. The estimate, Hunter?"

"It won't be necessary," he said evenly, slipping his hands into his trouser pockets.

He'd already gotten them. Well, that was quick. She hoped it didn't cost as much as she feared. Stupid, stupid, she thought. When would she learn to slow down? Reaching into her purse, she pulled out her checkbook, trying to remember exactly how much she had, and when she'd last reconciled her accounts.

It'd been a while. Her motto—make sure the checkbook balances only if she had money—meant that she rarely had to perform the task. "How much?" she asked, fishing for a pen in her huge, overloaded purse. "I'll just—"

"My insurance will cover it," he said quietly, reaching out to put his hand over the top of her purse. "Forget it."

His touch made her skin leap. It also increased her pulse rate uncomfortably. "I can't do that," she whispered.

"Sure you can." Bending around her, he opened her door, which served to remind her that he was in a hurry, and that he couldn't wait to get rid of her. "It's nothing, really," he said.

"Of course it's not. Not when you're late for your important meeting with the bombshell." Good Lord, where had that come from?

"Oh, *Hunter*!"

At the sound of a voice and the rapid clicking of heels, Trisha looked up to see none other than the just-alluded-to "bombshell" herself. Smiling, Sheryl waved a piece of paper and blew Hunter a kiss from a neighboring car. "Thanks so much for the tuition, Uncle Hunter!

Great-Aunt Gloria and Great-Uncle Patrick said you'd come through for me because you *always* come through for them, and they were right. Thank them for me, too, will ya?"

"I'll see you next quarter." Hunter waved back, then turned to Trisha with raised eyebrows. "You were saying?"

Oh, dear. She'd done it again. "I was saying I still have one foot left to stick in my mouth. Give me a minute and I'll be sure to do it right here so you can get some enjoyment out of it."

She had to give him credit, he didn't laugh at her. But he wanted to, she could tell. Unable to stand there feeling humiliated a second longer, she again turned away.

And again he stopped her. "Trisha."

Good Lord, the way he said her name, as if it were golden honey dripping from his mouth. It completely undid her. "No, please," she begged softly. "Don't say anything. I've really got to go. About the car—"

"I said, forget it," he said firmly.

Thankful, she slipped into the driver's seat. "For now," she agreed, because she so desperately needed to get away from him. "But I'm going to pay for that damage." She managed a smile. "Maybe I'll even throw in a car wash, to get any traces of lipstick off. It's the least I can do."

She shut the door, but he leaned down and tapped on the glass with a patient look on his face. With a deep breath, she rolled down the window. Casually, he rested his arms on the door and filled the window with his face, so close she could have moved a fraction of an inch and kissed him.

Light as a butterfly, he ran a finger over her lips,

then gave her one of his rare, heart-stopping smiles. "Pink today," he said, looking down at his finger.

"Wild fuchsia, actually."

"It suits you. You have an incredible mouth, Trisha. It makes me think of things I have no business thinking."

Good thing she was already sitting because her legs became useless.

His gaze roamed her features, then ran slowly down over her body, making her tingle in each place his eyes settled. When that gaze hit her exposed legs, covered only in sheer stockings, it heated, making her rethink her opinion about him never giving her a second look. He'd definitely just given her one. And a third look, and that third one had made taking another breath utterly impossible.

The sudden sexual tension had to be stopped, if only for health reasons. She'd suffocate this way. And her heart was pounding so fast, it was about to explode. "Great-Aunt Gloria and Great-Uncle Patrick—your parents?" she asked.

"One and the same."

The tone of his voice said back off, so did the sudden tension in his large frame, which served to rouse her hungry curiosity about him. "You never told me if you were close."

"No, I didn't."

Obviously, he had hoped she'd drop it. "Are you?"

"Depends on what you consider close."

"You're being purposely difficult."

He cocked his head. "I'm very aware of that fact. My secretary says I define the word. According to her, I'm also obsessively single-minded, a bit arrogant, and more than a little annoying."

Trisha smiled, thinking his secretary must be a keen psychologist, if not a saint. "You're changing the subject."

He sighed. "I'm trying."

"Do you give your parents money too?"

He shrugged.

"I thought you said you never let your family get the best of you."

"They haven't."

"Looks to me as if you're supporting the entire Adams clan," she said.

"I've got some extra money and they don't have any. Doesn't hurt me to help."

"You know something, Dr. Adams?"

His eyes regained their sparkle at her haughty tone. "What, Ms. Malloy?"

"I think you care a lot more than you let on. Which makes you kind and generous as well as difficult and annoying."

"What about arrogant?"

"No," she said slowly. "Not arrogant. Just basically quiet. Maybe even a little shy. People always mistake that for arrogance."

Startled, he let out a sound that might have been a muffled laugh. "My two ex-fiancées might disagree with you."

"*Two?*" she squeaked.

"If I recall correctly," he said dryly, "they both said nearly exactly the same thing when they left me. Cold, callous, and miserly with my affections."

They'd left *him*. "Did you love them?" she asked softly.

Again, she'd startled him. "I thought so at the time, but in retrospect, I decided I know little to nothing about that particular emotion. Nor," he added quietly, "do I want to."

Ah, now she understood, and her heart broke a little for him. "We're not all bad. You just can't ask everyone to marry you. You've got to be picky."

His mouth quirked. "*Now* you tell me." He sighed. "Marriage isn't for me. Getting engaged is just too damn expensive."

"You should have had them return the engagement rings."

A muffled sound that might have been an embarrassed laugh escaped him, and he avoided her gaze.

"You let them keep the rings," she said, not surprised. Hunter, a wealthy man in his own right, probably wouldn't blink an eye at the cost of an engagement ring. "You, ah . . . hadn't started wedding plans on either of those marriages, had you?"

"Maybe."

Now she understood. "And you covered the costs afterward, right?" That he didn't answer told her everything. "How much?"

"It's considered tacky," he said wryly, "to hound a man left at the altar with questions about how much he's spent."

"Oh, Hunter," she breathed, picturing this tall, proud man being stood up in front of his friends, his peers, his wretched family. "I'm so sorry."

"It's definitely for the best," he said with a small smile. "I could be shackled right now."

Yeah. And unavailable. Forget being sorry and thank God he'd been dumped. "That heart of yours is pretty big," she whispered. "Add that to kind and generous."

"Don't." His voice sounded rough with emotion. "I'm not kind, or generous."

"I think you are."

Reaching through the open window, he flicked at her long, dangling pink earrings. The pad of his thumb touched the sensitive spot beneath her ear and a shiver raced through her.

"You're wrong," he assured her, frowning with intense concentration as his thumb continued making soft strokes to her skin. "I just like to get everyone out of my hair. Nothing seems to do that quite like money."

He was making light of what he'd done, which touched her unbearably. She had to leave before she made a bigger fool of herself. "See you later, Hunter."

He didn't smile, but something passed between them, something unspoken, something hot enough to steal what little breath she'd managed to regain.

"See you later, Trisha."

Just as she turned to start the car his hand slid down softly over her hair, so lightly, she couldn't decide if he'd really done it, or if it was a case of her overactive imagination.

When she looked at him again, he'd straightened, his gaze impenetrable. "Try to stay out of trouble."

It coaxed a smile from her, and seeing this, he looked satisfied. Turning, he walked away, his long legs covering the ground with ease, his shoulders straight, his stride impossibly confident.

He'd never looked more distant, more unattainable. Didn't matter much, Trisha thought. No matter how many times she'd been forcibly reminded of their differences, she still wanted that man. Helplessly.

Trisha had no idea why her world suddenly didn't seem enough. She had the freedom that she'd yearned

for all those years while she'd been browbeaten and restrained by her aunt and uncle.

No longer did anyone tell her what to do, how to
dress, whom to associate with. It was wonderful, and
exhilarating. She had her own shop, which she ran as she
wanted. As her own boss, she came and went as she
pleased.

And she hadn't had to move once.

She'd had all this while scorning the things she saw
as tethers; things like marriage, having children, a man
to love. None of those were for her.

So what was wrong? Why wasn't this happy, carefree
life enough anymore? Why did she suddenly crave the
very things she'd always sworn to avoid?

It horrified her, these yearnings and needs she
couldn't control. Even worse, she had a terrible suspicion that they were due to Hunter Adams.

He drew her, and it wasn't simply because he was
gorgeous. Despite her jokes about his profession, his intelligence drew her. So did his quiet decisiveness, his
intuitiveness, his sensitivity. And then there was his surprisingly wicked sense of humor.

Too bad every little thing about her wrecked the
poor guy's peace of mind. Because of that, there was no
future for her with him except heartbreak and disappointment.

Celia, sensing her friend's melancholy, had splurged
and brought Trisha a present meant to cheer her up—a
basket filled with dozens of scented candles of all sizes,
bath oil, and a bottle of wine. For distraction, Celia had
insisted.

Trisha never drank, *never*, but Celia had wanted her
to consider this an experiment in relaxation.

Alone in her apartment that night, Trisha stared at

the pretty basket and its contents. With a fatalistic shrug, she set about preparing the bathroom. Finally, she stripped and sank into her tub. Glorious, scented bubbles rose, tickling her nose, and on every available surface candles flickered and glowed, casting a warm light about the room.

Nose twitching, Duff moved cautiously into the bathroom, slowly inspecting each candle.

"Watch that," she warned, when the sleek but none too graceful cat moved toward the bottle of wine. She'd opened it and set it on the edge of the tub next to an empty glass.

The cat moved closer, sniffing curiously.

"Duff," she said, watching him over the bubbles. "I'm not interested in a wine bath, or mopping the floor tonight. Go to bed."

The one thing that interested her tonight was peace and quiet. She wondered if she'd achieve it, or if her thoughts of Hunter Adams would hound her. Only if she let them, she assured herself, eyeing the bottle of wine.

"What the hell," she told Duff, who had jumped lightly on the edge of the tub to watch. She poured herself a glass. "How much damage can just a bit do?"

Apparently quite a bit on an empty stomach, in a lightweight woman who never drank. Within fifteen minutes of finishing her glass, Trisha had the giggles.

"Duff, sweetie . . ." Trisha squinted at the cat to make sure. "You've got four eyes." Laughing, she gestured with her glass. "Pour me another, honey, will you? But make it a small one 'cuz I'm driving." She laughed uproariously at her own joke. "Oh, dear, this stuff seems to have gone straight to my head."

Duff sat on his haunches and studied her seriously.

"Don't bother getting up, Duffy, I'll get it." Still

giggling, Trisha leaned forward and poured herself another glass, dribbling a good portion of it on the floor. "Darn." Frowning, she leaned over the tub to inspect her spill and, in the process, swished half of her chilled glass of wine on her bare breasts.

Sucking in air through her teeth, she looked at Duff. "That," she said slowly, trying to breathe, "was *not* a good relaxation method."

The second glass went down much faster than the first, but gave her the hiccups, which annoyed her. "This drinking thing is definitely not all it's"—*hiccup*—"cracked up to be." *Hiccup. Hiccup.*

Suddenly the smell of the bath oil made her feel a little sick. To top it all off, she'd forgotten to turn her heat on and her arms were covered with gooseflesh. "Duff, I'm thinking"—*hiccup*—"that this basket thing wasn't such a great idea."

Her stomach grumbled loudly. Duff straightened, alarmed, peering into the tub at her belly.

"Food," she decided. "I need"—*hiccup*—"dammit, that hurt. I . . . definitely need food." With the room spinning wildly, Trisha rose from the tub, sloshing water over the side. "Oooh, it's cold," she said, then sat back down with a splash. "*No way* am I getting out of here."

"Mew."

"Okay, okay . . . but first, just one more little itty-bitty glass of wine," she told the cat, who was studying her thoughtfully, as if she'd come from another planet. Chuckling at herself, she reached for the bottle . . . and knocked it into the tub with a splash.

"Oh, my," she squealed, leaping up. "A wine bath for a wino!" She grabbed the now-empty bottle, set it on the floor. Reluctantly, she pulled the plug and stood there watching in fascination as the bubbles swirled down the drain.

Then her world started spinning. "Whew!" she said, teetering wildly, befuddled. "I'm dizzy!"

"Mew."

Bed, she decided hazily. Forget the food, she needed her bed, and she knew she had to get there fast.

But suddenly she had four feet and no eyes. Well, hell, she thought. Nothing seemed to be working properly, including her legs. With the slow, calculated precision only a very drunk person can obtain, she stepped over the tub, carefully avoiding the flickering candles.

"No need to set the spacey scientist's house on fire," she told Duff, slurring her words slightly. "That might just be the icing on the cake, you know?" Carefully, she blew out each of the candles. "I still can't believe he got dumped"—*hiccup*—"*twice*. Those women must have been crazy."

She and Duff stared into the dying candles. Trisha's thoughts turned muddled. "*I* wouldn't have left him at the altar."

Duff backed away from her, curling his tail close to his body, giving her a hard, unsympathetic look.

"Smart cat, keeping your paws safe," she muttered, holding her hands way out in front of her as if to compensate for the fact that her world seemed to be revolving too quickly. "In my condition, I'm liable to trip over my own two feet."

Then she did exactly that.

From her sprawled, graceless position on the floor, she lifted up on her elbows and stared balefully at the cat.

He looked disgusted, making her burst out laughing at herself. "Didn't Aunt Hilda warn me?" *Hiccup*. "She must have told me a thousand times how I had two left feet."

Relaxation had finally come, and now her muscles seemed reluctant to work. But she could hardly stretch out wet and naked on the bathroom floor for the night. Besides, the floor felt cold, damp, and the cold seeped quickly into her exposed skin. She shivered.

"I'm really pathetic," she said to the cat as she hiccuped again. Sighing, she pulled herself upright, stumbled into her bedroom, and grabbed the first shirt she came across. Dragging it over her wet head, she fell damp and exhausted onto her bed.

She was asleep before her head hit the pillow.

In the bathroom, smoke was rising from the extinguished candles. Attached to the hallway ceiling, the sensitive fire alarm automatically responded to the harmless, drifting tendrils of smoke . . . and started to wail.

All the while, Trisha slept on.

EIGHT

Though it was only midnight, Hunter was deeply asleep, dreaming.

In space with his crew, he peeked out the window, down at Earth. Far below, scrawled in red lipstick over the planet were the words: SO SORRY ABOUT THE LANDING GEAR, HUNTER! I'LL BE HAPPY TO PAY FOR ANY DAMAGES. FONDLY, TRISHA.

Hunter groaned and turned over. The woman could wreak havoc on his world even while he slept.

He dreamed on.

He was back in his duplex in South Pasadena, music blaring, windows rattling. Trisha stood there smiling wickedly, holding up the black leather bikini. He tried to tell her he preferred the soft, ivory chemise, but she couldn't hear him over the annoying sound of the music.

But then he realized the noise wasn't music at all, and he stirred.

At the continued screech of the fire alarm, Hunter jerked in his bed, unwilling to let go of the dream.

He thought of Trisha's fuchsia fingernails, and wondered if she'd painted her toenails to match.

But the obnoxious shrill of the alarm kept bothering him until the dream faded completely. He sat upright in his bed. When he realized what the sound meant, he came instantly awake. Swearing, he threw back the covers, yanked on a pair of sweatpants, grabbed the portable phone by his bed, and strode to the door. Carefully, he laid a hand against it. Cool.

With his heartbeat echoing in his ears, he cautiously opened the door. No smoke, no flames, just the earsplitting sound of the smoke alarm.

Then he realized something terrifying—*his* alarm hadn't emitted the noise. It was coming from the floor above.

Gripping the portable phone, he sprinted through the house, tore out the front door. On the grass, he whirled back, craning his neck to stare through the black night at the upper level.

No light, nothing. But also no smoke or fire. Still, he had to be sure. Taking the steps three at a time, he knocked on the door.

But the knock faded away in the blare of the alarm.

"Dammit," he muttered, and tried pounding on the door, though he knew it would do no good. He peered over the railing—Trisha's car was parked in the driveway, perilously close to his own.

Where the hell was she and why hadn't she shut the thing off?

Her front doorknob turned easily under his hand, which only served to rile his temper further. She hadn't bothered to lock the door.

"Trisha?" he yelled. Nothing. Except, of course, the god-awful shriek of the smoke detector. That he still didn't see any sign of smoke or flames went a long way toward relieving him, but why hadn't she responded?

Calling her name, he moved through the kitchen, flipping on lights, then ran down the hall and tore into her bedroom. The light from the hall spilled into the room. The lump in the middle of the bed stirred at his voice. "Trisha."

Her wild hair emerged from the blanket first, then her confused, sleepy face. "God, what's that noise?" She covered her ears and stared at him.

"You're all right?" he demanded.

She blinked slowly, her mouth open slightly as she continued to gape at him.

What was the matter with her? "Trisha?"

She hiccuped, then squinted as she peered around her as if to make sure she was where she thought she was. "What are you doing in here?"

He didn't know whether to strangle her for terrifying him, or to yank her against him and never let go. But his aroused temper had him opting for the first. "It's your fire alarm," he said loudly, setting his phone on her dresser. "You've done something to set it off."

"I—" She broke off. "I did not. At least," she added in a mutter, "I don't think I did."

Shaking his head, he moved out of her room and back into the hallway. He stared up at the offensive alarm, then reached up and deactivated it.

Blessed silence filled the house.

The ache behind his eyes from stress and lack of sleep eased slightly. It came back in a flash when he thought about the deliciously rumpled woman in the bed in the next room, with her wide eyes that were always filled with a curious wonder, her pouty lips that seemed to beg to be kissed, her thick, luscious hair that never stayed in place.

She turned his world inside out.

How was she able to annoy him and arouse him at the same time? It had never happened before, and it alarmed him now, since he couldn't seem to control his response to her.

He wouldn't dwell on it, he decided. Not now, in the middle of the night. And he certainly wouldn't look at her again, not when he knew she was probably at this moment wearing some sexy little number from her store. Probably black, or red, leather or lace, he hadn't really checked when he'd been worried about a fire.

Now the only fire seemed to be in his groin.

As he reentered Trisha's bedroom he told himself she didn't drive him crazy on purpose. Yeah, and maybe the alarm had somehow just gone off accidentally.

Right.

He knew better, and because he did, he automatically took a deep breath, already on the defensive.

Which, it turned out, was completely unnecessary. Trisha had fallen back asleep.

Stretched sideways across the bed, half under her covers and half out of them, she slept on. He stopped in the doorway and let out a little noise of disbelief. "Unbelievable. Trisha."

She didn't budge.

Stirred by some uncontrollable urge he couldn't deny if his life depended on it, he moved forward, until his knees bumped her bed. In his dream, she'd been in black leather. Now, in the flesh, Hunter expected something equally erotic, certainly something frilly and feminine, something intended to entice and seduce.

She'd surprised him—again.

One long leg stuck out from the sheet, bare and smooth. Her covers, bunched at her waist, revealed her nightwear of choice, and it surpassed even the most sensual of dreams.

Far sexier than any black silk or lace, she wore a plain white cotton T-shirt . . . and she was cold. Oh, God. "Trisha."

For an answer, he got a soft snore. Feeling like a martyr, he leaned over her and pulled the covers up to her chin, tucking the blanket carefully around her.

She turned to her side, trapping his hand beneath her. "I'm sorry, Aunt Hilda, I'll do better next time," she murmured softly.

"Trisha."

"I promise—just please don't send me back."

The tense, desolate tone of her voice galvanized him. Hating that her dreams haunted her, he used his free hand to pat her shoulder. "You're just dreaming, Trisha." Then he stroked her hair. "Go to a happier place."

When she'd relaxed a little, he slowly pulled his hand free, heat spearing through his body when his knuckles accidentally brushed against a soft breast.

At that moment Duff stalked into the room, went still at the sight of him. Feeling like a molester, Hunter stepped back. Duff passed him, tail pointing straight up, chin lifted. Leaping onto the bed in one fluid motion, he settled proprietarily in the curve of Trisha's hip.

Trisha shifted, then whispered groggily, "Oh, Duff, you're so warm. For a minute I thought you were Hunter."

She thought this was a dream.

Shaking his head, Hunter turned from her. It was that or slip in beside her and give her some of the body heat just watching her had generated.

Because he still felt uneasy and unsettled about the

alarm, he walked through her bathroom, wanting to check each room. But what he found there told him he had no need to go farther.

Obviously, she'd had a hell of a time. Water was everywhere, beaded on the walls and the linoleum in the old, unventilated bathroom. The mirror was half-fogged. The scent of the bath still filled the room. Though the candles had all burned out and were cold, it didn't take a space scientist to figure out that they'd probably set off the alarm when she'd blown them out.

An empty bottle of wine lay on the floor, next to an overturned glass.

Frowning, he picked them up and set them on the counter. Without considering the wisdom of what he was going to do, he strode back into Trisha's dark bedroom. A beam of light from the hallway divided the room, highlighted the bed and her still form.

"Trisha."

No response, but at least now he understood why. She'd drunk herself into a stupor. Not feeling particularly sympathetic since she'd interrupted his sleep for the night—sleep he desperately needed—he reached out a hand to her shoulder and shook her. Actually, he amended to himself, she'd ruined just about every night's sleep since he'd first moved in, just because he couldn't stop thinking of her.

"Trisha, wake up."

"No."

Though her eyes remained firmly closed, she said this quite clearly, giving him the impression he'd actually woken her. "Yes." He had no idea if she did this sort of thing often, but the thought that she might was more upsetting to him than he wanted to admit. "We have to talk."

She clutched blindly at his arm, her grip tight, desperate. "I already ran the five miles, Uncle Victor. I'm too tired to do the push-ups and sit-ups. Please, I said I was sorry."

God. "Trisha."

"I won't make Aunt Hilda mad again, just don't make me."

His stomach clenched. Very deliberately, he sat on the edge of the bed. "No one's going to make you do anything," he assured her gently. "I promise."

Silence fell. He sensed the change immediately, knew she'd come fully awake by the sudden stillness and tension in her body.

"I found the fire," he said hoarsely.

"Fire?" she mumbled, pushing back her hair and blinking at him sleepily. "What fire? Hunter? Is that you?"

Who the hell else? "It's me." Without thinking, he leaned forward, braced himself on the bed, his hands on either side of her hips. "You were dreaming."

"No," she said flatly, shaking her head.

"You were," he insisted. "You said—"

"Please. I'm fine now."

"But—"

Again she shook her head, violently this time. Her hair flew, a strand clung to his slightly stubbled face. With a hand that trembled, she reached up and brushed it away. "Hunter."

The way she said his name made him want to groan, want to bend and take her mouth with his, then take the rest of her as well. He could still feel the warmness of her touch on his face, and he wanted more.

"Why are you here?" she whispered.

"The smoke detector went off, and I just reacted,

thinking there was a fire. I knocked—pounded—on the door, calling your name, but you sleep like the dead. And dammit, your door wasn't locked. You've got to lock it, Trisha."

"Fire," she said, moistening her lips, her eyes never leaving his face. "I remember you saying something about fire."

"I think the smoke from your doused candles in the bathroom set off the alarm."

"I'm sorry it woke you."

"Why didn't it wake you?"

She stared at him for a minute, then flushed. "I don't know."

"I do," he said quietly. "How often do you down an entire bottle of wine like that?"

"I didn't—"

"You could have drowned in that tub," he said swiftly, realizing just how angry he was. Dammit, didn't she care about herself at all? Still leaning close, he took her shoulders in his hands. "And I would have found you dead."

"No, I—"

Lifting her clear off her pillows, he pulled her upright, stared deep into her troubled, dark eyes. "Drinking is not the answer, Trisha."

"Dammit," she gasped, fisting her hands against him. "I know that." Her incredibly expressive eyes filled with tears. "My parents drank themselves to death. Do you really think I could do the same?"

For a minute he just stared at her. When he let her go, she sank back against her pillows. "I'm sorry, I didn't know."

"Of course you didn't." She laid her arm over her eyes. "You don't know much about me except that I drive you crazy, I play my radio too loud, and I won't move out of your house."

"And you rearranged my bumper."

Her lips twitched, but when she lowered her arm to look at him, her eyes remained suspiciously bright. "That too."

Guilt twisted at him, so did something much more potent, something he couldn't name. "Trisha—"

"No," she said quickly, propping herself against her headboard. "Don't say anything else. I want you to go now."

He'd judged her, quickly and harshly. But it didn't erase his worry for her. "Are you all right?"

"For a drunkard, you mean?" Her smile seemed forced. "Of course. How much trouble can I get into in the middle of the night?" At his raised brow, she rolled her eyes. "You'd better forget that question. Just go. Please."

He started to object, but what right did he have? Reluctantly, he rose, walked to the door.

"Hunter?"

"Yes?" In the dark room, he turned back to her.

"Did you race up here to rescue me, or your house?"

"You," he said without hesitation.

The light in the hallway highlighted the features of her face and he caught her small smile. "You even look like a hero, standing there like that, half-dressed." Her voice went husky. "You didn't put on shoes . . . or a shirt."

He felt more than saw her gaze run over the length of him, and his body responded so quickly, he felt dizzy. "I was afraid for you."

Some of the tension left her. "It's nice to know that. I'm sorry I woke you."

He nodded, turned to go, needing to get out.

"I didn't drink that whole bottle of wine," she whispered as he stepped out of the room.

Unquestioningly believing her, he closed his eyes and went still. Self-disgust filled him.

"The rest spilled in the tub," she explained quietly. "It's why I got out—well . . ." she added wryly, "that and the fact that since I hadn't eaten, and I never drink, it went straight to my head."

Why did being wrong have to hurt so badly? he wondered. And why did it have to be so hard to apologize? Or was it just this woman, and the fact that he had to work so hard to resist her?

"Are you ever going to try again, Hunter?" she ventured quietly. "Try again to trust a woman?"

"No." But he moved back into her room, again coming close to her bed. "I judged you," he said softly. "And it was wrong. I'm very sorry, Trisha."

Lifting a shoulder, she shrugged lightly, as if to say, Don't worry about it. You do it all the time.

It made him feel sick.

She was used to being harshly judged, and from the snippet of the dream he'd heard, he knew that went back several years. His heart twisted. No one deserved that, least of all this woman who wouldn't purposely harm a fly. "It matters," he said in a low voice. "It matters a lot, and I won't do it again."

"That's some promise."

She doubted his ability to keep it, and he couldn't blame her. "I mean it."

"Nothing's changed, Hunter. I'm still going to annoy you at every turn."

"You don't."

"Don't lie. Please, don't lie."

"You don't," he insisted, not surprised to find that he spoke the utter truth. "What annoys me is the way I react to you, when I don't want to. And it's not a matter of trusting you, Trisha. I just don't like to lose control, and I always seem to around you." There, he'd said it. He'd been brutally honest, as was his custom. Even though he knew, despite their assertions of the contrary, that women didn't really want honesty.

But he kept forgetting that Trisha Malloy was unlike any other woman he'd ever met.

"You resist it too much," she said. "Why can't you just go with it?"

Because it would terrify him. All his life he'd failed in relationships. This time would be no different. He could provide well, as in the case of his family, but he didn't seem to have much else that interested a woman for long. "Because there's no point."

Though he couldn't see her exact expression, he sensed her immediate withdrawal. "Of course there's not," she said softly. "Because there could never be a future with a woman like me. Not for a man like you. Is that it, Dr. Adams?"

"No, that's not it." His hands fisted at his sides as he dropped his head between his shoulders and studied his bare feet. He didn't understand what Trisha did to him, why she affected him so.

Women were like his projects—they came into his life for a short period of time, he enjoyed them, they left his life. On to the next project. Rarely did he *look* back. He'd certainly never *gone* back.

An uneasy feeling stirred inside him. Trisha was different, startlingly so. She didn't seem to fit into any area of his neat, meticulously planned life. In fact, she regularly destroyed any sort of structure he had, sometimes with just a look.

As she was doing now.

Even in the dark, he could sense her swirling emotions. And he knew with every fiber of his being, she wanted him to kiss her into oblivion again, every bit as badly as he wanted to. But he couldn't, not yet. "It has nothing to do with who you are, or what you do, Trisha."

"Then what is it?"

"It's me," he admitted tightly. "It's the man I am, it's what I do."

"That makes no sense," she said, twisting her hands in the sheet and pulling it up to her chin. "What's so wrong with the man you are that you can't let yourself enjoy a . . ."

She trailed off and he smiled grimly. "Enjoy a what? What exactly is this between us?"

Mute, she stared at him.

"See?" he pressed, giving in to the urge to be close and sinking to her bed to sit at her hip. "Even you know better." He reached for her hands. "This *thing* between us has a life of its own."

It's uncontrollable, Trisha thought. And it scares us equally. Me, because eventually he'll walk away, and him, because he's afraid he won't be able to.

But she wanted him, had to have him. And she knew how badly he wanted her. Dressed as he was, in just lightweight sweatpants and nothing else, there was little he could hide from her. He was magnificent, she thought, with his vital and able body so nearly bare for her to see. It made her ache, the rippled strength, the easy, graceful way of moving he had. The hard planes of his chest, the flat belly, his long, powerful legs, the unmistakable and impressive hardness between them. Desire slammed into her just from looking at him.

He made her feel needy and strong at the same time, and she'd never in her life felt that way. Nor had she ever wanted anyone quite as desperately as she wanted him.

Well, she'd just have to make sure she didn't restrain him in any way, make sure he felt he could just turn it off at any time. Though it would hurt, it was the only way to play this, or she'd lose him. "Haven't you ever had an affair before, Hunter?"

He looked startled. "I—uh . . ."

With a little laugh, she squeezed his hands. "It's a simple question. Yes or no?"

"Yes," he said through his teeth.

"Then what's the problem? Are you telling me you analyzed each one so carefully beforehand? Worried and fretted about its demise before it even got started?"

"Yes." But his lips curved. "See? We're too different." His eyes deepened, darkened, and he leaned closer. "Send me away, Trisha."

"No," she whispered, pulling her hands from his and wrapping her arms around his neck. "No," she said again. "Not tonight." And she kissed him.

NINE

At the first contact of her lips on his, Hunter's entire body stiffened with shock. She took her mouth away, trailed it over his clenched jaw. "Just go with it, Hunter," she murmured throatily. "Let it take us."

"For how long?" he demanded softly as his hands came up to hold her upper arms.

"Do you need a game plan?" But she sighed when he remained silent. "Of course you do. Fine," she whispered, fighting his resistance and pressing her face into his neck to inhale his delicious male scent. "For tonight, then. Just tonight."

"Just tonight?"

No. "Yes." Then she held her breath, waiting. God, it would kill her in the morning, to let him go. But for all his careful plans and strategies, he was like a wild bird who couldn't, wouldn't, allow himself to be contained. To try to hold him would end this before they'd even started, and she had no intention of letting that happen. Not when she was this close.

Give him his freedom, she thought desperately, and

he won't run away. He wouldn't be able to, she assured herself, because he felt this pull between them every bit as strongly as she did. "Just for tonight, Hunter. Please . . ." Her lips moved over his face. With her teeth, she gently pulled on his ear.

He groaned, then gently eased her back, following her down, down, down on the bed. "We shouldn't."

"Yes, we should," she gasped as he let the full length of his body slide against hers.

Sinking his fingers into her hair, he stared into her eyes as if unsure what to do next.

"Kiss me, Hunter," she whispered, arching up to him just to feel his body tighten against hers. "Just start there and see what happens."

She didn't know what she had expected, a slightly fumbling, unsure kiss . . . an awkwardness . . . ineptness.

She got none of those things.

Warm and tender and erotic, Hunter's masterful lips seduced hers, kissing her with a promise of things to come, giving without reserve, in a way she was beginning to anticipate. Giving in to the impulse, she ran her hands over him, reveling in the deep, needy sound he let out.

Dragging his mouth from hers, he kissed a trail down her throat, buried his face in her neck. "Mmmm." Warm, wet openmouthed kisses were planted in the curve of her neck, over her shoulder. "God, you smell good."

She clutched at him, helpless to do much else as passion and desire raced through her. Her blood pounded in her veins, roared through her heart as the anticipation and hope built to an almost unbearable level.

His hands slid around her waist, so gently she melted

against him. Again, his mouth captured hers, in a sweet, searing kiss that quickly escalated until they both panted breathlessly, their hands grappling as they blindly reached out to touch.

Hunter lifted his head, pierced her with eyes so painfully green she felt she could see all the way to his soul. "I don't want you to regret this," he said, his voice gravelly.

"I won't."

"Trisha—"

"I'm a big girl, Hunter, capable of knowing what's right for me. And this is it." But he didn't kiss her again. Desperate, she pulled at him, but he resisted. Something wild pummeled her suddenly, a fear so great it stole her breath. He was going to leave her, just stand up and go when she needed him so fiercely she ached with it.

Her hands gripped his shoulders, jerked him back down next to her. "Please, Hunter," she whispered, pulling him closer, closer still, until their bodies lay side by side, limbs intertwined. In case he still wanted to move away, she fisted her hands in his hair. "Don't go."

His arms slipped around her once again, tightened on her. "I'm right here." He kissed her again. "I'm right here," he repeated softly, his mouth fusing with hers, building and building a pressure inside her, sending her to a place beyond reason.

Her urgency seemed to spark his own. She felt his hands smooth down her spine, over her bottom, cupping and squeezing gently, before gliding under her T-shirt to touch skin to skin. "Please," she heard herself whispering. "Oh, please."

He stroked her back with terrifying tenderness, his eyes alight with a desire she'd waited so desperately to see. She heard his harsh intake of breath as he shifted over her, pressing hips to hips, felt the muscles in his shoulders bunch as he moved down. Then, through the thin cotton of her shirt, he nuzzled her, gently nipping with his teeth.

Her hands ran over his shoulders, his chest, over the sleek muscles of his back, pressing, urging. In response, his body moved against hers in a rhythm as old as time. Long, lean fingers skimmed up her thigh, raising the shirt as they went, over her hip, past the indentation of her waist, high on her ribs.

Trisha held her breath, watching his bent head drink in the sight of her. Gently, he cupped a breast, his thumb gliding over the hard, aching tip. Her head fell back against the arm that held her to him, as an intense, sharp need left her limp. Then he took her pebbled nipple into his mouth, his tongue slowly circling it teasingly, until she thought she would die of the pleasure. When he sucked her into his mouth, hard, she felt nothing but a bright burst of raw desire.

Hunter looked at her flushed face, at her glorious body spread out before him. He'd been trying to regain some semblance of control, but it was slipping, badly. Drinking in the sight of her body, bathed softly in moonlight, almost undid him. The virginal white of her T-shirt flirted with the creamy, soft texture of her skin. Her full, curved breasts, still damp from his tongue, made his mouth water, the lush flare of her hips made his fingers itch to touch. White bikini panties covered her feminine secrets. Demure, yet incredibly sensual. The powerful combination electrified him. "Trisha, you're so beautiful." The choppy little sounds escaping her lips were the sexiest he'd ever heard. Lightly, gently, he cupped her.

She whimpered his name, gripping him tight.

His control shattered.

He wrapped Trisha in his arms, pressed her hard into the bedding, and crushed his mouth to hers. Kissing her with a heated thoroughness didn't diminish the need, instead it fueled it. So did the endearingly awkward way she held him so close he could hardly breathe. He didn't mind one bit. Reaching down, he slid his fingers under cotton, through soft curls, and found her slick and hot for him.

She gasped. Her fingernails dug into his shoulders.

He thrust gently into her and groaned at the exquisite wet, velvety feel of her. Tight, he thought, so unbelievably tight. Lightly, but sure and utterly relentless, he moved his fingers until his name tumbled from her lips, her voice low, shaky . . . anxious.

"It's all right," he whispered against her skin. "I want to feel you explode, Trisha. Come for me." Then he kissed her fiercely, while his touch had her quivering, panting. In the next instant the delicious tension in her shattered as she surrendered with a wordless cry of wonder.

He held back, waiting until she was lost in the storm, trembling and shuddering, before he patiently started again, dipping his head to lave at her breast.

Trisha could hardly stand it. Drowning in the endless waves of pleasure, she couldn't catch her breath. Within seconds she felt herself trembling again, so close, so very close. . . .

Above her, Hunter went still.

With hungry, desperate desire pounding her, blood raging through her veins, Trisha couldn't think beyond her own need. She gripped his arms. Beneath her fingers, she felt him quiver and knew he was holding back purposely. "Hunter."

Lifting his head, he stared at her, his mouth still wet from kissing her breast. "The alarm," he said thickly.

She let out a little laugh. She'd heard bells, too, they'd been ringing in her head ever since he first kissed her so hotly. "It's not real—" She stiffened.

They were real. She heard them now. Only it wasn't a bell, but a siren, loud and getting louder.

With regret and an unleashed fire burning in his eyes, Hunter's gaze ran down the length of her exposed body. "They're coming here."

The siren came closer, got louder.

"No," she whispered. "No!" Reflexively, she clamped her thighs tight, holding his hand against her.

Hunter sighed and dropped his forehead to hers. "I'm sorry, Trisha."

She didn't relax her thighs, still imprisoning his hand against the hot, desperate part of her that needed him. She couldn't. A sound of wordless remorse left his lips as he tenderly pried open her legs. With a last, soft kiss to her lips, he sat up, slowly, regretfully.

From her window came the flash of red-and-white lights. The siren wailed once loudly, then cut.

"But . . ." Her hips were still mindlessly rocking, her body still tingled and ached and wanted. . . . Dammit, she felt like crying.

Then Hunter reached for her, ran the pad of his thumb once lightly over her lips before pulling her shirt back down to her thighs. "Someone must have called them when the alarm went off," he said quietly, his voice not quite steady as he stood and walked to the door.

From far below came the sound of voices.

"I'll go tell them what happened."

Still sprawled on the bed, she could only stare at him.

Was she the only one rendered positively speechless by what had just happened, by what had almost happened?

No. Even in the dark, she could see the blatant evidence of his own raging desire.

"I still want you," she whispered.

"Trisha—God, I'm sorry. But I've got to go before they come up here looking for the fire."

"Come back?" she whispered, but he'd turned away and didn't hear her. The skin of his sleek back glistened, and she knew no matter what he wanted to think, he wasn't immune to what had taken place between them.

She ached to touch him.

"Try to go back to sleep," he said quietly, then turned back to her. "It's late."

Her gaze rose to his face and she realized the awful truth. *He wasn't coming back.* Already, he'd reestablished his distance. Her only comfort was that barely checked hunger flickering in his eyes.

Fine, he wanted to suffer alone, she'd let him. Pride refused to allow her to beg him. But it was difficult, knowing he was leaving, and that every inch of her still trembled for his touch. "Good-bye, Hunter."

For one last interminable moment, he looked at her. Stark need shimmered there, *for her.* So did something else, something deeper. Basic affection, yes, but even more. It thrilled, even as it terrified. She opened her mouth, then shut it again. Anything she said now would have him bolting, running scared.

"Trisha."

Her name spoken so sweetly made her heart thump. But then his lashes lowered, and he masked his emotions from her. "Good night," he whispered, and he left.

He still feared this, she realized. The loss of control wasn't acceptable to him.

Sleep, he'd suggested.

"Yeah, right," she muttered with a shaky sigh. "I'll be able to get some sleep now." Trisha punched her pillow, burrowed deeply into her blankets, and tried not to remember what his mere touch had done to her. Or how good his body had felt against hers.

Tried not to think about something even more disturbing: She was falling in love with him, if she wasn't already there.

"So," Celia asked with a sly smile when Trisha made it into work the next day, "did the basket do the trick? Did it do something for you?"

"It did something, all right." It had given her a ridiculous headache, among other things. Trisha slipped out of her coat and moved into the shop. The scent of lilacs and wood filled the air. Music drummed, pulsing pleasantly. From deep inside, an inner peace worked its way through Trisha's tense body. Her slight hangover began to fade.

Here, at least, she could relax.

She hoped.

"You don't look so well," Celia said, moving close, looking worried. Her hair today was red, still spiky, with an interesting white streak down one side. Her one-piece bodysuit, jet-black and vinyl, matched her black-lacquered fingernails. Somehow, in the way only Celia could carry off, she looked gorgeous. "What's the matter, honey?"

"Late night," Trisha muttered, shrugging off the concern. It just might make her fall apart.

"You didn't sleep well?"

She hadn't slept at all once Hunter had left her, her

body so charged and fired up, it wouldn't, couldn't relax. Finally she'd hugged her pillow tight, imagined it was Hunter's long, lean, hard body, and dozed fitfully until dawn.

His car, bent fender and all, had been gone when she awoke.

"Trisha?" came Celia's worried voice.

"I'm fine." She sighed, turned, and faced her closest—and only—friend. Celia had been there through thick and thin—always. Even when Trisha had moved from California early on, they'd kept in touch with constant letters. In late high-school years, when Uncle Victor had been reassigned and Trisha had moved back, their friendship had continued as if they'd never been separated. Never in Trisha's life had making friends been easy, *never*, except with Celia. "The basket was wonderful, and it definitely worked—for a while."

"Awhile?"

Trisha took a deep breath. "Until Hunter arrived, found me passed out cold in the bed with the fire alarm blaring."

"Oh my God." Celia, a woman *never* startled or ruffled, stared at her, eyes huge. With unmistakable hope, she asked, "Did he take advantage?"

"Celia! I wasn't drunk."

"I didn't think you were," Celia said faithfully, dropping all pretense of trying to sort through a box of new merchandise. "What happened? Did you do the deed?"

"Celia."

"Sorry. No, I'm not. Tell me."

"I guess the smoke from all the candles set off the alarm, but I fell asleep so fast . . ."

"You were very tired."

"Thanks," Trisha said with a tight smile. "But I think I made a fool of myself when I did wake up."

"No, I'm sure you didn't."

To stall, Trisha bent, dipped into the new shipment, and pulled out a midnight-blue boxer pajama set. "Actually, I did. I pretty much threw myself at him."

"Really? Does the scientist do other things as well as he kisses?"

Trisha carefully hung up the pajamas and dug farther into the box. "How do you know how he kisses?" she asked, amused at the salacious look on Celia's face.

"I saw you the other day in your closet of an office, remember? I saw that dreamy, 'I'm lost in lust' look on your face. Besides, with a body like that, it'd be a shame if he didn't know how to use it."

Oh, he knew how to use it, all right. Her legs went weak just thinking about it. "The point is," Trisha said primly, "I threw myself at him. I don't think he's used to that."

"No man in his right mind would complain."

"Maybe not," she conceded. "But Hunter is different. He seems to have trouble with my lifestyle."

"Well, then he doesn't know you very well, does he?" Celia reached for Trisha's hand. "It bugs you. What he thinks gets to you."

"A little."

"It shouldn't."

"I know, I can't seem to help myself." Trisha shrugged. "I think about him far too much."

Celia's eyes softened in understanding. "You're falling for him. You're falling for a man like you've always said you never would."

"No."

" 'A steady relationship is not for me,' you've always

said. You've avoided them like the plague. Only a date here and there, and only when I beg you." Celia looked at her, amazed. And concerned. "And now, out of the blue, you go for the very opposite of yourself—an uptight, conceited intellectual who—"

"He's not conceited."

Celia gave her a long look. "Fine. But he is—"

"I know, I know." Trisha sighed. "He's—" What had his secretary said about him? "Single-minded, a bit arrogant, and more than a little annoying. But it's all just appearance, Celia. I know it is. It's a cloak he wears, almost as if it's protection. And think about it, a man like that would need protection. He's affluent, wealthy, well-known. He's probably hounded regularly."

"Yeah," Celia said dryly. "I bet it's real tough looking as good as he does, and having money too! How awful for him. My sympathies."

Trisha ignored that. "Beneath that cool, distant exterior, there's so much more. He's intelligent, funny, sensitive. Passionate."

"Oh, man," Celia breathed, staring at her. "You're gone. Really gone."

"Yeah," Trisha said miserably, dropping the lacy garment she was holding to cover her eyes. "I am. And it's just awful."

"Don't worry. If he hurts you, I'll kill him."

Trisha laughed weakly. "My hero."

"Are you sure, Trish?" Celia asked suddenly, grabbing her hands, staring into her eyes. "Is he really the one?"

Another weak laugh came from her. "I'm sure he wouldn't think so."

"It's what you think at this point that matters."

"He's the one," she whispered.

"He's very different from you, from what your hopes and dreams are," Celia pointed out needlessly.

"My hopes and dreams were to be left alone to be as I wanted to be. But now . . . well, I'm still wanting to be as I am, but I don't think I want to be alone. Does this make any sense?"

"I just don't want to see you let down. Are you really, really sure?"

"I'm sure," Trisha whispered. "I can tell he has feelings for me, deep ones he won't give in to this easily. I'm not sure why, but he won't."

"Maybe he's been hurt," Celia suggested reluctantly. "Or maybe he just isn't the type to let go easily. He does seem to be really disciplined."

"Yes," Trisha said, thinking of how he'd been able to walk away last night when she'd been a quivery mass of nerve endings. Then she thought of his deep eyes and their swirling secrets. She'd sensed his hurt. "But he isn't cold. Far from it."

A customer walked in then, and desperately needing to stop thinking, Trisha moved to offer assistance. "I just need to forget this madness," she whispered over her shoulder to Celia. "It's a dead end for me, no matter how much I want it."

Her face tight with love and worry, Celia watched Trisha walk away. "Your entire life up until recently has been a dead end, honey. It's time things went your way. For once. You deserve it. You can't just forget about him."

Then she sighed, knowing Trisha wouldn't act on this advice herself. A smile touched her face. "But I can act on it for her," she murmured.

TEN

She'd been perfect, the stuff dreams were made of. Jaw tight, temper questionable, Hunter strode down the long corridor of NASA, for the thousandth time dwelling on what had happened with Trisha a few days earlier.

He'd wanted her, badly. Still did. Any normal man would have gone back for her, he thought, disgusted with himself. But he wasn't normal. Not by a long shot.

Cowardice.

That's what held him back. What he wanted with Trisha couldn't be easily relegated to the file in his brain labeled TENANT. Or even FRIEND. No, what he wanted was much more complicated than either of those. Nor could he wish her to the back of his thoughts, acting on the principle of out of sight, out of mind. She stayed front and center inside his head, where she could worm her way into his heart and soul.

He couldn't have it. They were a poor match, and he hated poor matches. He liked order, daily planners, thinking ahead. Organization meant everything. Trisha liked chaos, going with the flow, and being impulsive. The word *organization* wasn't in her vocabulary.

It wasn't meant to be.

It's not that he didn't like her as a woman. Hunter sincerely liked women, but tended to go out only sporadically, choosing someone who wanted a pleasant diversion and nothing more.

Trisha was definitely more than a diversion. Tempting as she was, she also meant trouble, and he always avoided that.

He had to come up with a plan so that he didn't have to see her, hear her, crave her. Only one way to do that, he thought dismally. He had to sell the house. She'd hate him for it, yet he could see no other way.

But God, he wanted her.

Walking through his office door, he picked up his phone messages, walked to the window, and stared down into the courtyard below.

Peace. Calm. Joy. His work gave him these. And since he was about to start working, he could relax. Then he looked down at his messages and tensed up again.

His mother had called. Her message read: *Your father is at it again. If I don't kill him by the time you get this, make sure you talk to him and tell him I won't consider coming back until he straightens out.*

He sighed and hoped it wasn't too late to stop his mother from committing murder. Why, he wondered as he moved toward his phone, couldn't his parents just simply stay away from each other?

It wasn't just his parents that had him riled. It was everything. His neat little world suddenly seemed . . . not so neat.

Just the day before he'd come out of the house to find the trash can knocked over on his front lawn, Duff sitting daintily in the middle of the grass, snacking on leftovers. Trisha had rushed out of the house, obviously late as she struggled with several boxes, slipping on her heels as she ran.

With a small, apologetic smile, she'd shooed Duff away and had prepared to clean up the mess. He'd pulled her up, taken her boxes to the car, and cleaned up Duff's mess himself.

He'd ended up with squashed banana on his black silk shirt, much to Trisha's muffled amusement. With some desperate, ridiculous need to wipe that laughter from her face and replace it with half of the hunger he felt, he'd hauled her against him, backed her to his car, and kissed her until they broke apart, panting.

Right in plain sight of anyone passing, yet at the time he couldn't have cared less if the entire neighborhood drove up to cheer him on.

The aftermath of that one violently tender kiss left him unable to emerge from behind his desk that entire day.

Then, just the night before, while trying to read through several trade journals, flecks of plaster had rained down on him. Above him, to the beat of the loud music, he could hear Trisha dancing and singing at the top of her lungs.

All he'd been able to do was wonder what she was wearing, and wish Eloise had installed a peephole of her own so that he could watch.

There'd been no more lipstick messages, but he had to deal with the indignity of finding his mulberry bushes trimmed into the shapes of bunnies, apparently courtesy of Trisha plying the new gardener with fresh chocolate-chip cookies.

With her joyous, carefree ways, she'd wormed her way right into his life, even as she drove him to the brink of insanity.

Restlessness forced Hunter to push himself hard, then when he could still think, he pushed harder. His staff, long used to his perfectionism and dedication, didn't blink an eye at his increased hours. Nor did they dare comment.

Except his secretary. Entering his office, Heidi handed him the report he'd requested. Then stood there.

"Is there something wrong?" he asked, putting the file down when it became apparent that she wasn't leaving.

"I was going to ask you the same thing."

Hunter sat down and stared at her. "What?"

"I know this is none of my business," she began. "But we've worked together a long time, and well . . ."

"Just tell me," he said gently, thinking she was working herself up for another pregnancy leave.

"Okay." Heidi fidgeted her fingers. "I'll just tell you. I'll just spit it out—"

"Heidi, *please*. Just say it."

"Rumors are flying, Dr. Adams," she said quickly, with sympathy in her gaze. "I wouldn't have said anything at all, but you're expected at the charity event tonight, as is everyone else you know, and well . . ."

"Well what?"

She made a face. "I'm sorry," she said carefully. "But I feel I must warn you. Speculation is rampant, fueled by the fact that you were seen racing after some woman the other day in the NASA parking lot."

Oh, perfect. Closing his eyes, he pinched the bridge of

his nose with two fingers and struggled to shrug off all the tension.

"Just the fact that the unflappable Dr. Adams was caught running was amazing enough, but the woman . . . when you so rarely are seen showing emotion to one . . . I'm sorry," she said again, blushing. "But I wanted you to know."

"I see." What the hell was he supposed to say? That he had a new tenant, a wild, crazy, beautiful, sweet woman who was slowly driving him insane? That she somehow drew out the worst and best in him at the same time?

That he couldn't stop thinking about her?

"It's just that you never lose your cool," Heidi said, breaking the silence. "You're always so in control."

Maybe, but he'd lost it, hadn't he? "Thank you, Heidi," he said calmly. "Tonight should be . . . interesting."

"To say the least."

Hunter realized exactly how much she'd risked to warn him. After all, they didn't talk often. He typically wasn't even in his office much, spending most of his time in the lab. But he appreciated what she'd done. "I guess I'm the main topic in the secretarial pool these days."

"Yes, you beat out Dr. Jansen, who was caught in the buff under his desk with Dr. Phillips." Now she grinned, more relaxed. "Don't take it personally, Dr. Adams. The men are just jealous, and the women . . ."

He was sure he didn't want to know the rest. "And the women . . . ?"

"They just wished that they were on the receiving end of the Devil's attention."

❦————❦

Once Trisha came to the startling if not slightly terri-fying realization about her feelings for Hunter, every-thing made more sense.

Or at least it did until she came home one evening at the end of the week and found a realtor scoping the place out.

"Excuse me," she said to the small, weasely-looking man in a red jacket holding a clipboard, pacing out the perimeter of the property.

He lifted his nose from his board. "Yes?"

"What are you doing?"

He was rather young. And given the way he eye-balled her, allowing his gaze to rove slowly over Celia's latest creation—a deep green jersey mini-suit—she fig-ured his interest in measurement extended to more than the property.

Long before he'd finished introducing himself as Sam Walters, real-estate agent, Trisha started to sweat. Her lungs labored, and her knees felt weak. It was a familiar panic attack, one that she hadn't had since the last time she'd been forced to move, but she knew how to deal with it.

All she had to do was lock her knees and remember to breathe.

"I'm measuring the size of the lot," Sam Walters said with a smile meant to charm. He moved closer. "You live here?"

"*Why*—" Her voice sounded so hoarse, she had to clear her throat and start over. "*Why* are you measuring the lot?" Breathe, she reminded herself as she felt the panic surge, double in force. *Breathe.*

"Trisha."

She whirled at the sound of Hunter's voice and

dragged in a deep gasping breath. He stood there, having just gotten out of his car. She had been so intent on the way her heart was racing, on her feelings of betrayal, fear, worry, and a million other things, she hadn't even heard him drive up.

Though they'd seen each other on and off during the week, they hadn't really spoken since that night of the fire-alarm incident when he'd . . . Trisha swallowed hard, shoved away the heated memory, and faced the horror of the moment. By now she could feel the sweat pooled at the base of her spine, could feel herself start to hyperventilate. "You've decided . . . to put . . . the house on the market." The last part of the sentence came out in one breathless rush.

Hunter frowned with concern and stepped closer.

The agent shifted on his feet, ears perked up. Probably hoping for a scene, Trisha thought with disgust, and promised herself she wouldn't give him one. But breathing became more difficult at the shuttered truth in Hunter's eyes.

"Please, answer me," she said, struggling to take in more air.

"You're so pale. Are you all right?"

She added fury to her present panic. Except for that kiss in the driveway, he'd avoided her after giving her the most erotic experience of her life. Now he was going to take away the only home she'd ever had, and he wanted to know if she was all right. "Are you . . . or are you not putting this place . . . up for sale?"

His frown deepened. "Trisha."

The weasel Walters divided his attention between the two of them, moving his head back and forth as if watching a tennis match. Trisha wanted to smack him, but the loss of oxygen had spots swimming before her eyes. "Just tell me," she said to Hunter as softly as she could—not difficult when her lungs had refused to work. "Is it true?"

Hunter's eyebrows came sharply together as he stared at her. "I'm thinking about it."

"I have a lease." Dammit, her voice shook. "You can't break it. Eloise promised me."

"Mr. Walters, thank you for your time. I'll speak to you another day," Hunter said, dismissing the other man.

The weasel's nose twitched, sensing defeat. "But—"

"I'll be in touch," Hunter said firmly, his eyes never leaving Trisha's. "Again, thank you."

Trisha watched the real-estate agent walk down the long drive, lined with the rosebushes she herself had planted last spring, and concentrated on dragging air into her aching, shaking body.

Hunter was going to sell.

As Walters drove off she took in the old but absolutely charming white house and experienced a pang so sharp she bit her lip against it. The pain reminded her to suck in some more air, which was a good thing since her vision had started to waver with the lack of oxygen.

"Trisha."

Selling. Moving. Packing. Losing all sense of place, of being. Could she do it again?

No. *No*, she thought with welling panic, she couldn't.

From far away, she heard a soft oath, then felt a hand grip her upper arm. Next thing she knew, she was sitting on the porch step, her head thrust between her knees and held there by a firm hand. She struggled violently.

"Stay still, dammit," Hunter said in a low, rough

voice. His hands held her. "And breathe, for God's sake."

She tried, and made a horrendous gulping noise that would have immobilized her with humiliation if she could have thought beyond her own misery.

"Again," he demanded, and she realized from her limited view from beneath her knees that he'd sat down next to her. Vaguely, she wondered about the obviously costly trousers he wore, and what sitting on the step was going to do to the fabric. He'd have an expensive dry-cleaning bill.

Great. Between his car and the damage to the bathroom and kitchen floors, she didn't owe him nearly enough already.

"Keep breathing. . . . That's it," he said quietly when her next breath came easier.

"Let me up," she snapped.

"Well, you're talking, at least."

The hand that held her head down loosened its hold to stroke her hair, soothe the taut muscles in her neck and shoulders, reminding her yet again of another night when he'd touched her with that same tenderness. She gulped in more air.

"Much better," he said softly, encouraging.

When she could, she lifted her head, torn between embarrassment and bitterness. "I'm fine." But her hands shook as she smoothed down the skirt of her suit, which had risen high on her thighs.

"Are you really?"

That was it. Exploding off the stairs, she wavered for a minute, flinging off the supporting arm he had placed around her waist. "No, actually I'm *not* fine," she said, her heart still racing, her palms damp. In the face of her anger and betrayal, the panic had receded for now.

Hunter's hands were tucked casually in his trouser pockets, his feet planted firmly apart, as if ready for battle. His voice came quietly. "What's the matter, Trisha?"

She wanted to cry, laugh, scream. "You know what's the matter. You're going to sell, after you said you wouldn't."

"I never told you I wouldn't."

"You moved in here," she pointed out. "I thought that meant—that you wouldn't— Oh, hell," she said softly, pushing her hair from her face. "I'm sorry. I . . ." She looked wildly about her, in desperate need of an escape. Her bike, lying against the side of the house, seemed the perfect getaway vehicle. "I've got to go."

Without a thought for the jersey suit and heels she was wearing, she yanked the bike away from the house and got on.

"Trisha, wait."

The fitted military jacket didn't pose a problem, nor did the short, snug skirt. But her open-toed shoes gave her a rough moment when they got caught on the pedals. In less than two minutes, however, the house—and Hunter's anxious, angry voice—had faded from view.

Moving wouldn't be so bad, she reassured herself as she hit her stride, peddling along the quiet streets of South Pasadena. After all, she should be used to it.

And maybe, just maybe, if she got real lucky, the new owners of the duplex would want a tenant.

Hunter Adams would be just a bad, distant memory. *Right.*

Hunter stood there for exactly half a second, rooted in shock at Trisha's abrupt departure, before he jerked his keys out of his pocket and ran to his car.

He had absolutely not a clue as to what exactly he'd just witnessed, but he'd bet his last dollar it had been a panic attack. "Crazy woman is in no condition to be riding a bike," he muttered, quickly unlocking the car with the intention of following her.

"Excuse me. . . ." a female voice called from the street. "Wasn't that Trisha going off on that bike?"

Hunter paused as a woman with bright red hair laced with a white streak shut the door of her car and hastened up the walk. He recognized her immediately from the day he'd visited Trisha's shop. It'd been the day they'd shared that first volcanic kiss.

"Hello, again," she said, waving as she came closer, the silver jewelry jangling in and on various body parts.

Hunter was positive that the last time he'd seen this woman, her hair had been jet-black. "Yes, that was Trisha," he said hurriedly, still wanting to go after her, though he knew she wouldn't welcome the intrusion.

"She looked upset."

Hunter didn't answer, but shut his car door with a sigh. Trisha had enough of a head start now that she could avoid him forever if she wanted to. He'd have to wait her out, and hope she didn't get herself killed while she rode off her demons.

Celia was staring at him, and for the first time in he couldn't remember how long, he felt like squirming.

"What happened?" she asked, putting her hands on the hips of the shiny black cat suit she wore.

He wanted to tell her to mind her own business, but the torment he'd seen in Trisha's eyes haunted him. "I told her I might sell."

Celia's gaze turned from pleasant to deadly solemn in less than a heartbeat. "I see." Without a word, she headed back to her car.

"Wait!" he called. "Please, wait."

"I'm going after her," Celia said, not stopping. "I've got to find her."

"*Please*," he said again.

She stopped but didn't turn around. "She's got to be terribly upset."

"She's more than just upset," he said, feeling helpless. "I think she had some sort of panic attack."

As Celia swore vehemently, Hunter knew that he had to be missing a big piece of the puzzle that made up Trisha Malloy.

"Tell me why what I said upset her so much."

"That should be obvious." Celia glared at him. "She doesn't want to move."

"I understand that much," he said sardonically. "She's told me often enough. What I meant was, tell me *why* it matters so much. It's just a house. And a run-down one at that."

"What's it to you?"

He couldn't answer this question, only knew he was suddenly driven to understand the woman he knew he'd inadvertently hurt. "It's important."

She glanced anxiously down the street. "But Trisha—"

"Is long gone," he assured her grimly, every bit as worried as she obviously was.

Celia sighed and looked at the house. Finally, with a resigned shrug, she walked back up the drive, her four-inch heels clicking. She stepped onto the patio, where she sat on the wooden bench beneath the bay window.

"Might as well kill two birds with one stone," she said to herself.

"What?"

"Sit," she said, patting the bench. "Sit, Dr. Adams, and listen."

He gladly complied.

ELEVEN

Two hours later darkness had fallen. Hunter still sat on the bench in front of the house, waiting. Fretting. Worrying. Seething, but not at Trisha.

Celia had left, but only after exacting a solemn promise that he would call her when Trisha returned. There'd been a heavy warning in her voice, one that he understood all too well.

She expected him to make it all better. The responsibility didn't daunt him; he was more than used to NASA and his family expecting miracles from him. "Call Hunter, he'll fix anything" seemed to be a motto the people who knew him adopted.

But this was different. Trisha had no family or work ties to him. She certainly hadn't asked for his help, had in fact done everything in her power to avoid doing so. Which somehow only made the compulsion to solve the problem all the stronger.

But what exactly should he do?

She should have been back by now. Something had

happened to her, something horrible. She hadn't been thinking clearly, she'd been riding recklessly.

His fault, dammit, his fault. He should have gone after her immediately, should have kept her here and forced her to talk about the house. Instead, he'd let her leave. If something had happened to her, he'd never forgive himself.

With the intention of calling the police and every hospital within twenty miles, he stood and walked to the end of the porch.

Then he went completely still as relief flooded through him.

The wheels on her bike squeaked; he knew this because she often rode it to the store and he could hear her coming from a quarter of a mile away. He heard her now.

The minute she turned into the driveway, he was there, holding the bike as she got off. Her hair looked like an explosion in a mattress factory, wild, long strands everywhere. Her eyes seemed huge in her pale and drawn face. Huge and red.

Dammit, she'd been crying. His gut jerked. "I've been waiting for you."

Her shoulders automatically squared against him, making him regret his words. Why didn't he just say he had been worried sick? That he cared what happened to her and wished she hadn't run off? Women liked that sort of thing, he remembered belatedly, then wondered why the hell he was worried about pleasing her. He was mad as hell at what she'd put him through. "Are you all right?"

"Of course." With that unusually cool, distant tone, she turned from him and walked toward the outside stairs.

"Wait."

She didn't, but he wasn't surprised. He was beginning to know her better than he'd planned to, and she was stubborn as hell. With three easy strides, he caught up with her and gently took her arm, turning her to face him. "Please, Trisha. I want to talk to you."

"No."

One simple word, yet with layers of meaning behind it. Mostly panic. He understood some of that now, thanks to Celia, and his fury choked him. He wanted, quite badly, to go find her uncle and show him exactly what he thought of his child-rearing techniques. Though Hunter had never used physical force to prove anything, he found he wanted to do so now, quite violently. But that wouldn't help Trisha.

"Come inside," he said, trying to propel her resisting body toward the house.

She dug in her heels and he swore he could see steam coming from her ears. Frantically, he searched his mind for an incentive—women liked incentives, didn't they? "I'll make you dinner," he offered quickly. "You must be starving after all that riding."

She looked at him as if he were mad, and in truth, he felt that way. "No," she said.

"Trisha, I—"

"I'm going upstairs now," she said carefully, through her teeth. "I want you to go away and leave me alone."

"I'm sorry, I can't do that," he said with regret.

"Yes, you can!" she cried, pulling her arm free. "Just go on with your cozy little neat life, the way you always do. And leave me a-alone!"

Her voice cracked on the last word, breaking his heart, and he reached for her again. She tried to evade him, and for a moment they stood grappling under the glare of the porch light.

Hunter heard the footsteps first. A couple, out for an evening stroll, watched them curiously as they passed, obviously drawn by the raised voices.

"Go away," Trisha whispered to him in a hiss as she raised a hand and smiled at their audience.

"Not until we talk," he said between his teeth.

The next-door neighbor chose that moment to pull up his driveway, the headlights of his car illuminating them. Trisha closed her eyes and took a deep breath.

In that flash of time Hunter could see her clearly, the paleness of her usually flushed skin, the near translucence of her eyelids, the faint purple circles beneath them. Sick, he lifted his hands from her shoulders and sighed.

Mutinously, she stared at him, looking so damn vulnerable it made him ache for her. "Okay, that's it." As gently as he possibly could, he took her hand and tugged her close. "Inside. Your place or mine?"

"Not with you. Not again." Her jaw tightened and she tried to pull away, but he held firm.

"To *talk*, Trisha."

"I don't want to talk."

"I realize that," he said conversationally, pulling her as nicely as he could toward the stairs. No, he decided, changing direction in midstride, not her place. Too many memories for her there. He changed directions, heading to his front door.

"If you don't let go of me, I'll scream," she warned.

She would, too. His heart aching, for he hated what he had to do, he stopped and turned to face her. "Go ahead, it might make you feel better."

"You have no idea what will make me feel better. I—"

"I know why you're upset, Trisha. I know why you flipped out about my selling this place. We've got to talk about it."

"No, no we don't." She took a deep breath, visibly tried to pull herself together. "Look, I'm sorry about tonight, okay?" Now she smiled, and he could only call it such because she showed her teeth.

"I've been working a lot," she said. "And not sleeping as much as I should . . . the usual working-girl stuff, that's all. I'm just cranky." She backed up several steps.

"You are not just cranky," he said. "You had a panic attack."

Now she stepped off his porch, still walking backward. "It's all in how you perceive it," she told him. "And I—"

"Did you hear me, Trisha?" he asked her softly, not chasing her. "I said *I know*. I know what's wrong with you."

"Yeah. I need to go to bed." Nervous energy practically rose off her in waves. A bubble of laughter escaped. "Alone," she added swiftly.

Time to play the ace. "*Trisha.*"

"Good night—"

"You moved eighteen times in eighteen years."

Turning dead white, she stopped short, nearly tripping. "What—what did you say?" she whispered.

"You were forced to wear the god-awful secondhand clothes your aunt purchased for you. Ugly clothes she purposely bought too big because you matured so early. She needed to make certain you were so unattractive, no one would look twice at you. She was afraid you'd become easy otherwise." God, the expression on her face killed him. As he thought this she whirled, poised to run.

"It didn't matter, though," he said hoarsely to her stiff, proud back. "Because you just stuck out all the more. Moving so constantly didn't help."

Trisha froze, so still she could have been a statue.

"When you'd cry at night, your aunt would spray holy water on you and command you to stop being evil and wanting material things."

Her shoulders hunched defensively, and he longed to hold her, but he couldn't give in to the urge, not yet. "They stopped giving you a separate bedroom, so you couldn't escape, making you sleep in the living room where anyone could see you. You never had even a small space you could call your own."

Until now, he thought, with a sharp pang of regret. Trisha still didn't move.

"College was good," he continued quietly. "You stayed in the dorm, though you had to work night and day to come up with the tuition money since you had no family willing to help. Directly after graduation, you came here, mortgaged yourself to the gills, and bought your store. Your aunt and uncle nearly had heart failure, but you haven't had to move since."

"You realize, of course, I'm going to have to kill Celia now," she said finally, in a voice so low he almost missed it.

Even now, in a moment of deep anguish, she could resort to sarcasm. He guessed it was her only defense. "She was worried sick. Now I know why."

"Lots of kids have it worse."

Not many, not even him. "What you've done with your life is pretty terrific," he said, daring to come up close behind her. "Running a successful business—"

She let out a short laugh. "You haven't seen the books."

"You've made something of your life," he said softly.

"Stop it." Slowly, she turned to face him, her dark eyes shimmering with so much pain it stole his breath. "Just stop it. So you know why I'm so attached to this place. Big deal. Doesn't help much in the face of your plans . . . and don't you *dare* tell me you're going to change them because of what Celia told you. I wouldn't believe you."

He had no idea what to say or do next, and the helpless feeling ate at him.

"I'm going in," she said quietly, crossing her arms over her middle. "I'm cold and I want to change." With a quiet dignity that tugged at his heart, she attempted to smooth down her hair as she walked past him, her chin high. The forest-green suit she wore was made of a clingy material that emphasized each graceful swing of her hips. Watching her walk caused the predictable male physical response, but for Hunter it went far deeper than that.

She dressed the way she did because for the first time in her life, she was free to do as she pleased. Free to wear clothes that fit her body, free to pick and choose what she did with her time and with whom. So much about her suddenly made sense now, and for the first time since she'd literally fallen into his arms weeks ago in his bathroom, he felt as if he knew her, understood her.

"Celia's dead," she was muttering as she moved. *"Dead."* Then: "Gossip with her again, Dr. Adams, and I'll have to kill you too," she called over her shoulder.

She already was killing him, but it was a slow death. "I guess our talk is over."

She lifted a hand and kept going. "Good guess."

"You can't avoid me forever," he said.

"I can try."

"Trisha—"

"No." She stopped abruptly, her back still to him. "I . . . can't do this," she whispered.

He moved up behind her, careful not to touch. It was hard, when he yearned to do just that. "Can't do what?"

"This." Still not facing him, she gestured wildly, which he took to mean him, this, that, everything.

"I hate what you know about me," she said, tipping her head way back and studying the sky. The ends of her hair drifted across the small of her back. The smooth white column of her throat drew him. So did the plunging neckline of her trim jacket. And though the last thing she needed at that moment was an aroused male, it was exactly what she got.

"I hate what I know, too, because it makes me ache to go back and fix it all for you. But I can't, Trisha. It's done, and you're grown. But I'm not sorry I know," he murmured. "I can't be, when now I can understand so much about you."

"Don't you see?" she asked, turning to him. "That's exactly what I'm talking about. You know everything about me and I know next to nothing about you. It makes me feel at a disadvantage."

Which she also hated. Well, he understood that well enough. He wished he could just do as she obviously wished he would—leave her alone. But for some reason, he couldn't. He couldn't let her go. Nor could he draw closer. "I'd never use what I know to hurt you. *Never*, Trisha."

Her mouth tightened. "Soft talk won't get me to break the lease."

"I didn't mean—"

She started walking toward the stairs again. *Hell.* "Trisha, please. Come back."

"Stay out of my life, Hunter," she said unevenly. "I mean it." But she didn't. Good Lord, she didn't. More than anything, as irrational as it seemed, she wanted him to hold her, to wrap those wonderful arms around her and never let go.

"Trisha."

The way he said her name had her eyes stinging. But she didn't slow down, couldn't.

She'd gotten to the bottom step when he said, "God, Trisha, you're tearing me apart."

That makes two of us, she thought, faltering slightly before regaining her footing. *Definitely two of us.*

Without another word or glance, she climbed the stairs and went directly to her bedroom, where she stripped down, dove under a blanket, and covered her face with a pillow.

She refused to cry.

The next morning Trisha stretched, but without much satisfaction. She hadn't slept a wink, and it didn't take a genius to know why. She'd told Hunter to stay out of her life. Would he listen? Had she meant it?

Of course she had. But goodness, it shouldn't hurt so much, should it?

Bravely, she checked the front yard. No "For Sale" sign appeared. But she didn't allow herself a sigh of relief, for it would be short-lived.

It was only a matter of time, she told herself, and tried not to panic. It couldn't be as bad as it sounded. She might find another place she liked just as much. Maybe she'd get used to the idea.

Then she tried not to think about Hunter, and how her feelings for him complicated everything. And how mortified she felt over what Celia had told him. Celia. She'd managed to avoid her so-called friend's calls last night because she intended to have it out with her in person.

But she'd never be able to face Hunter again.

Suddenly she wanted to take back those words she'd flung at him. Anger and humiliation had caused her to say something she hadn't meant. If only he weren't so perceptive, so startlingly intuitive . . . such a damn good kisser.

After showering, she headed down the stairs, dressed for work in a purple lamb's wool sweater and a matching short suede skirt—yet another of Celia's designs. Because of the sleepless night, she was running later than she would have liked, and she hurried, head down, her shoes clunking noisily on the wooden stairs.

Just her own dumb luck, she supposed, that she should run smack into a set of warm, solid arms.

She squealed in surprise.

Hunter caught her barreling weight with the grace with which he did everything. The tentative, disarming smile he sent her turned her heart to mush.

She barely checked the urge to throw her arms around his neck. Instead, she stepped back and smoothed her skirt. He followed the movement with his gaze, then cleared his throat, his smile fading.

In the time it took her to blink, he'd responded to her coolness and had distanced himself as well. "How are you this morning?" he asked, polite as ever.

Her jangled emotions made it difficult to respond. So did the carefully masked concern on his face. He looked mouthwateringly perfect in his sport jacket and fitted trousers. She'd never seen a man wear clothes quite so well. "How am I?" It wasn't in her to be less than honest. "Embarrassed," she admitted, deciding to keep the *confused* and *aroused* part to herself.

"Don't be," he said softly. "We all have something in our past."

"Yeah, but we don't all have that little something aired out in the open."

"Is that what's bugging you most?" he asked in astonishment. "That I know?"

"That," she answered evenly, "and the fact that I don't know much about your past."

"It's really boring," he said, surprising her by reaching out to touch her cheek softly. "And anyway, I've got to go, I've got a meeting."

"Oh, well, then." Trisha smiled and tried not to be hurt about his lack of interest in revealing a thing about himself. "Have a good day."

"You too." He tossed his keys in the air, catching them easily. She recognized the gesture as a nervous one and wondered what the stoic Dr. Adams could possibly be nervous about.

"Could we . . . get together tonight?" he asked, unusually hesitant.

A date. Well, finally! He'd completely forgiven and forgotten she'd ordered him out of her life. Now, if she could just be so lucky as to have him not discuss her past or sell the house, she was home free. "That would be nice," she said in a huge understatement, wondering frantically what she would wear, where he would take her, what they would do. *If he'd kiss her again.* "I'd love that, actually," she blurted out loud without meaning to.

"Good," he said with some relief, obviously completely unaware of where her thoughts had led her.

Good thing she didn't blush easily. "Because we didn't finish our discussion last night. . . . We have things to resolve."

"To resolve," she repeated slowly, her euphoria fading as understanding dawned.

"I didn't mean to hurt you by putting the house up for sale," he continued quietly. "That's the last thing I want to do, but—"

"You want to talk."

"Yes. Talk."

Not a date, she thought. All he wanted was to finish their talk—the talk she had no intention of finishing. Oh, she was an idiot. Such an idiot, in fact, she had to laugh. It was that or cry, and crying wasn't even an option. Not with Hunter standing there looking at her as if she were a basket case.

"I'll be home around six-thirty," he started, then broke off abruptly at her darkening expression. "Is that a bad time?"

Oh, the man was a prize. A Ph.D. in whatever it was he did in space, but he didn't know the first thing about women. "For a *discussion*?" she asked sweetly, her hands on her hips. "Yes, actually, Dr. Adams, it is. If you'll excuse me . . ." Annoyed at herself, and more hurt than she wanted to admit, she brushed past him and headed toward her car.

He followed her, his brow furrowed in befuddlement. "What *is* a good time?" he wanted to know.

At her car, she fumbled through her purse for her keys. Why was it she could never find them when she wanted to make a dramatic exit? "I'm not really sure."

He straightened and gave her a long look, as if he'd just figured out she was out of sorts. "Why is that?"

"Well, because I don't run my life on a schedule as you seem to." Darn it, *where were her keys?*

"Trisha," he said softly, turning her to him. "What is wrong?"

"Nothing—" she started, but he shook his head sharply. "Nothing and everything and I don't know," she said, exhaling painfully. "Oh, God. Fine. I thought—I thought you were asking me out."

"On a *date*?" He looked startled.

"Yeah. How ridiculous, huh?" She pushed at him, useless when the man stood solid as a wall. "Please, just go to work."

He squeezed her shoulders gently. "You thought I was asking you out." He marveled, shaking his head at himself. Then he looked at her, his eyes deep and spilling over with laughter and affection. "I didn't realize you would accept."

"Didn't realize—" She clamped her mouth shut to keep from sputtering. What did he think after the other night, that she let every man who saved her from a fire touch her like that?

"The other night," he said carefully. "Before the fire department came, I told you we couldn't do this. You said—"

"I know what I said." *For tonight*, she'd told him. And fool that all men were, he'd believed her. "I wasn't asking you to marry me, Hunter. Just a date."

"I know. I'm sorry, just forget—"

"Go to work, Hunter, you're safe from me. Just stop looking at me."

He didn't stop, he only moved closer.

She backed up. "Don't touch me, either," she warned when he reached for her, suddenly grinning a little. "And stop laughing at me."

"Is that all?" he asked with a straight face. "Don't look at you, don't touch you, and don't, for heaven's sake, laugh at you?"

"That's right." Good Lord, she sounded ridiculous, but false pride refused to let her take back her words. "I can't think when you do any of those things."

His lips twitched and she folded her arms over her middle. "I mean it."

"Of course you do," he murmured, leaning close to plant his lips on hers. It rendered her dumb, so he took advantage and did it a second time, wetter, deeper, with far more hunger and heat.

"I said don't look at me," she whispered when she could breathe again.

"I didn't," he whispered back, his eyes laughing now. "I had my eyes closed. And I didn't touch you either." Guilelessly, he lifted his hands. "See?"

No, he hadn't had to touch her. Not when her traitorous body had leaned of its own accord against his long, harder one. "Go away, Hunter."

"I'll see you tonight, Trisha," he whispered, and slid his lips over hers once again in a light kiss that shimmered with promise and passion, before turning and walking away. "We'll make it a date."

He whistled as he confidently strode off, not bothering to wait and see whether she would accept his offer. She guessed he knew her better than she wanted to admit. He hadn't waited, because he knew she'd say yes.

She frowned and rubbed her chest where it pounded excitedly from just a simple kiss.

Damn him and damn her, but she wanted another.

TWELVE

Luckily for Trisha's life, driving had become second nature. Her thoughts, far from the road, raced. She felt exhausted and bone-deep weary, both from too many emotions and too little sleep.

But suddenly things seemed different, less dire. Even more surprising, she felt so strangely light, so amazingly unburdened. Nothing had been resolved, and certainly Hunter could still decide to sell the duplex and walk right out of her life, but the weight of her past didn't seem so overwhelming anymore.

For some reason, having Hunter say the horrors out loud had put things in a less painful perspective. The past could no longer hurt her. The only thing that could do that now would be Hunter walking away before they even started.

What was and could be between them held her thoughts now, and she instinctively knew, if Hunter let it, it would be the best thing that had ever happened to her.

She opened Leather and Lace, having beat Celia in

for the first time all week. She flipped on the lights, the heater, and some music before settling herself to open her new shipment. She stared down into the box, stunned.

The local distributor she'd used was not new. In fact, they used him frequently, and often the shipments came with bonus items as a thank-you for the business. This shipment, given what had caught her eye, was no exception.

She'd gotten a bonus, all right.

Just then Celia walked into the shop, her hair a startling platinum blond. "Hey, sweetie. I've been worried sick. I called all night and—" She broke off. "You look like hell. Face drawn and stressed and—are you *laughing*?"

"Yes," Trisha said, shaking with it. "But not at you. Come in here and look at this stuff. And don't remind me that I'm mad at you. We'll discuss that whole issue later."

"But why didn't you return my calls? I was worried—"

"Celia, what the hell is this for?" From the box in front of her, she pulled out a leather whip.

Celia let out a startled laugh as she studied their new stock. "Why did you order that?"

"I didn't, and in case you're interested, I had my hands full with the man you decided to spill my guts to. Thanks a lot, by the way."

"He deserved to know, Trisha. He looked sick, thinking he'd done something to set you off."

"Well, he did." Trisha dug deeper into the box, past a chain-link bra-and-panty set. "He's thinking about selling the duplex, but I suppose you figured that out by yourself."

"Trisha." Celia laid a hand on her arm. "I think he's as scared as you are."

"Of what?"

"Your feelings for each other."

Trisha dropped a selection of silk scarves and looked at her friend. "I'm not afraid."

"You're both scared silly and you know it. He wants to run like hell, yet he can't because he wants to stay at the same time. It's like going on a date in quicksand, you know?"

"Great. Now you tell me." Trisha rolled her eyes. "I have a date with him in the deepest, wettest quicksand you've ever seen—tonight."

Celia smiled. "Bring these." She pulled out several beautiful scarves. "You can always tie each other up so neither one of you can run."

Trisha laughed, a little uneasily. "I don't think he planned on asking me out, not really." This was the embarrassing part, but what the heck, she couldn't humiliate herself more than she already had the day before. "I sort of corralled him into it, to tell you the truth."

"Then you'll really need these." She dropped the scarves into Trisha's lap. "Hold him hostage until he admits his feelings."

She'd need more than silk to hold that man down. As huge and powerful as he was, she couldn't imagine anyone keeping him against his will.

"Oh, good Lord, is that a— *it is*." Gingerly, Celia reached into the box and lifted a wooden paddle. "Wow. Heavy thing, isn't it? What did you want this for, besides the obvious, I mean."

Trisha had to laugh at the speculative look Celia gave the paddle as she weighed it carefully in her hand. "I didn't order these things. They came extra. And oh, my God—look at this." She held up a pair of handcuffs.

"Oooh," Celia said, convulsing with laughter. "Give me a pair. I've got a date tonight, too, and he's willing as hell."

"You're sick." But for the next half hour they pulled out an assortment of sex toys, giggling and snorting hysterically like a pair of schoolgirls.

They laughed all the harder when their first customer appeared, caught a look at some of the devices in the box, and wanted to know how much they cost.

All in all, it was a surprisingly good day, made all the better for Trisha when she got home and still no "For Sale" sign had been posted.

Feeling generous toward the world, and more than a little smug since she'd had a stellar day at the store, her mood was light. It would have been even lighter if she'd remembered to stop at the post office to mail back her shipment of wicked toys, but oh well.

Organization was not a strong suit.

Before she got out of the car, she twisted in her seat to grab the box in question, unwilling to leave it in her car overnight. Just her luck, they'd get stolen and she'd have to report a list of missing sex toys.

Laughing a little at herself, Trisha went inside her apartment. Not messy, yet far from spotless, it definitely had that lived-in look. Books and magazines littered the coffee table, but why clean them up before she'd finished reading them? In the middle of the chaos lay Duff, fast asleep on his back, spread-eagled.

"Just like a man," she told him, scratching his belly until he awoke to rub his head affectionately against her.

With over an hour to kill before her so-called date with Hunter, and her mood so light and unexpectedly carefree, she looked around for something fun to do. "I need to try something different," she said aloud as she raided her disarrayed hall closet.

Duff followed curiously.

"Something challenging, something fun. Something that I won't have to think about. They're in here somewhere . . . ah, here they are."

Triumphantly, she held up a pair of Rollerblades. She'd purchased them several months before and had never quite gathered the nerve to try them. She had that nerve now. "Hey," she said to a clearly startled Duff, "anyone who can sort through that box of sensual stimulators can certainly learn to Rollerblade."

Duff stared at her doubtfully and walked away. With a shrug, Trisha padded herself up and headed out. On the driveway she carefully put on the skates and took a deep breath.

Wobbling, she headed down the slight slope. At the bottom of the driveway, as if standing watch, sat Duff. As she headed toward him, gathering momentum, she waved her arms and murmured, "Oh, dear."

Gaining more speed, she yelled, "Move, Duff!"

He crouched, but because of his complete faith in Trisha, he didn't move.

"Get out of the way!" she called to him, wildly waving her arms now, ankles trembling with the effort to stay upright.

Too chicken to fall on the ground, and even more afraid to keep going, Trisha did the only sensible thing.

She closed her eyes and screamed.

Duff screamed back and, at the last instant, raced up the closest tree.

Trisha, not as lucky, crashed directly into the trunk of the tree, which rained leaves and twigs down onto her.

It took her a minute to regain her senses, and while she was doing so, she lay still on the sidewalk, sprawled gracelessly on her back, her eyes closed from the brightness of the setting sun. A mental inventory told her nothing was broken—except her pride.

A car engine revved close by, then the vehicle pulled into the driveway a little recklessly. The door slammed, footsteps slapped on the ground as they ran to her.

Leather shoes, Trisha reflected, her eyes still closed. Which meant only one person she could think of. She braced herself for the impact of that incredible voice.

"My God, Trisha." It was low and concerned, and every bit as sexy as she remembered. She heard his knees hit the ground beside her, pictured the new holes in his pants, and marveled at the amount of dry-cleaning damages she owed this man.

"What the hell did you think you were doing?" he demanded as his large, gentle hands touched her.

Hysterical laughter threatened. Blading definitely was not one of those things that was as easy as it looked.

"You're crazy," he muttered, his fingers skimming down the backs of her legs. "Absolutely bonkers. Which makes me bonkers. God, Trisha. Say something."

That's when the giggles hit her—the kind that couldn't be subdued.

"Please talk to me." His hands shifted to her arms, carefully checking each limb, each joint. "You're shaking."

Yeah, she was shaking, she was laughing so hard she couldn't talk. Would she ever stop making a fool of herself in front of him? Unable to help herself, she continued to choke on laughter until her ribs ached. Images came to her, of all the idiotic things she'd recently done—falling into his arms while he'd been going to the bathroom, ruining the kitchen floor, accidentally setting off the fire alarm. She remembered the indescribable expression on his face that night as the sound of approaching fire trucks interrupted their lovemaking.

Hunching herself into a ball and grabbing her stomach, she let loose with another round of laughter.

Hunter swore, a little desperately. His hands, low on her back, obviously checking for broken ribs, stilled. "I don't think anything's broken," he said in a hoarse voice. "But I'm calling an ambulance anyway."

"No," she gasped, getting ahold of herself with some effort. Lifting her head, she wiped her tears of mirth away. "Did you see it, Hunter? Did you see that terrific slide into the tree? Come on, admit it, I'm the most graceful person you know."

His eyes narrowed dangerously. "You're—you're *laughing*."

"Well, I certainly wouldn't be crying, not now." She sniffed and ran a finger beneath her eye, checking. "My mascara is going to run before our date."

"You're *laughing*." He shook his head. "I was sick . . . and you're laughing."

"You have to admit, it was pretty funny. I smashed into the tree at full speed."

He looked at her for a long moment, then sighed. "Trisha, you're going to be the death of me, I swear it." He swiped a hand hard over his face. "Did you know you just about gave me a heart attack? I'm cruising down the street and I see you slam yourself face-first into a tree. *God*." He rubbed his chest and she suddenly cheered even more.

"You care about me," she said, grinning from ear to ear.

He looked at her, shaking his head. "I have absolutely no idea why. I've never been so attracted to someone who laughed at me constantly."

So attracted. Her heart soared at the telling words, but she faked a wince. "That tree . . . *was* pretty hard," she said softly, wrinkling her forehead as if in sudden pain. "I think I'm feeling . . . dizzy."

He looked at her doubtfully. "Are you?"

"Yeah. *Real* dizzy." For effect, she swooned a little.

Though he dropped the doubtful act, he clearly saw right through her. Still, he opened his arms. She went willingly, sighing as they folded around her with delicious strength and warmth. He pulled her close and she ducked her face under his chin, pressing against his throat and neck, inhaling deeply.

"Trisha?"

"Hmm?" She was in heaven.

"You're not hurting one little bit, are you?"

"No. Not really," she murmured, hugging him close. His arms tightened imperceptibly.

"You're crazy, you know that?" he demanded in a low whisper. "And you're slowly driving me into that same state."

"I gave you an out," she whispered. "I told you to stay out of my life, but you didn't listen."

"I'm going to live to regret that decision, believe me. But later, not now." His head dipped down, a fraction of an inch from her lips, and her heart started beating hard and fast in anticipation.

"Just a date," she said softly. "It's just one little date." But oh, she wanted so much, much more. "You can handle that, can't you?"

His lips met hers in answer.

"Mew."

She'd forgotten Duff. Pulling back with dismay, Trisha glanced upward at a second, more pitiful cry. "Oh, no, Duff. I'm sorry, boy. Come down here."

Hunter rose spryly and shook his head as the badly frightened cat backed higher up the tree. "He's not coming down, Trisha. He's really scared."

Trisha had gotten Duff the day she moved into her apartment. They were a team, a family, and she had to get him down safely. "Then I'll have to go get him," she declared, reaching her arms up for the lowest branch of the towering oak tree.

"You can't do that."

In exasperation, she turned to Hunter, who stared at her with a mixture of pique and sympathy. "Why not?"

"Because you're still wearing Rollerblades."

That was easily fixed, and she bent to unlace them, but he pulled her back up. "No way. You'll likely kill yourself on my property. Come on now, move." He set her aside and reached for the branch.

"*You're* going to get him?" she asked.

"Yes." With weary resignation, he shoved up the sleeves of his shirt. He hauled himself up that first branch with a lithe ease that startled her. Before her eyes, he nimbly climbed the tree, reaching Duff in less than a minute.

It took a great deal of balance, and more than a few muttered curses when a frightened Duff lashed out with razor-sharp claws, but Hunter finally managed to coax the cat into his arms and down the tree.

Trisha grabbed Duff, hugging and kissing the humiliated cat before letting him go. She raised shiny, grateful eyes to Hunter, looking so lovely, his breath caught.

"Thank you," she said quietly, beaming.

She still wore her helmet and pads, though she'd removed her skates. When he thought about her crash into the tree, and how serious it could have been, his heart rate sped up. Or maybe it raced in reaction to the way she was looking at him.

Heat filled her gaze as he watched, and again his heart reacted. Definitely the way she looked at him, he decided. Which didn't make it any easier to accept. He didn't want to be affected by this woman.

He could control this. He didn't have to feel this way.

Oh, sure. And he didn't need air to stay alive either. "Promise me you aren't going to ride hell-bent for leather down that driveway again."

"At least not until I learn how to brake," she said solemnly, lifting her hand in promise as she looked at him. Then she gasped. "You're hurt. Oh, I'm sorry." She grabbed his arm and carefully pushed up the sleeve, which had fallen over several nasty, bleeding cuts.

Her hair fell over him, smelling clean and flowery. Her warm breath tickled his skin. Her concerned murmur made him feel more wanted and cared for than he'd felt in a long time. He was falling for her, he realized, quite hopelessly. And right then and there he knew he had to get away, now, before things got any further out of control.

Trisha lifted her head and smiled gently at him.

Run, he thought. *Run now.*

"Come inside," she said. "Let's clean these up."

Before his brain could protest, his feet had taken over, following Trisha up the stairs.

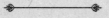

There were more than just a few cuts, Hunter realized as Trisha led him down the hallway of her apartment. Each of them had made itself known by the time she'd sat him down in her bathroom and pulled out a first-aid kit.

As she dabbed antiseptic on his arm, carefully watching his face for any sign of pain, she asked, "You okay?"

"It's just a few cat scratches, Trisha. I'll live." But the ones on his chest, the ones she hadn't yet discovered, were burning like wildfire. "I'll just go downstairs and shower and change," he said casually, but she put a hand to his searing chest to stop him.

He couldn't control his wince.

"Wait a minute." She reached for the buttons on his shirt.

Grabbing her fingers, he said, "I'm fine. Let me just—"

"Hunter," she said quietly, moving from his side to stand between his outstretched legs. "The blood is starting to seep through your shirt—oh, Hunter," she breathed, gingerly pulling the material sticking to his skin. She leaned close and peered down his shirt.

Her wild hair dusted his face, the scent of her teased his nostrils. She stood between his tensed thighs. Seemingly of their own volition, his hands came up to bracket her hips. At the unexpected contact she started, and stared at him, mouth open slightly as if she could hardly breathe.

"Duff got you good," she whispered unsteadily.

"Trisha," he said, just as unevenly, "let me up." He'd clean himself up in his own place, knowing if he let her touch him, he'd lose his already very tenuous grip on his control.

Just a date, he reminded himself. One little date.

But her nimble fingers again reached for the buttons on his shirt, releasing them one at a time. When she freed the last one, she spread the material wide, exposing the expanse of his chest to her gaze.

She drew a sharp breath.

In spite of the considerable discomfort of four bright, deep gouges running from collarbone to belly button, his body tightened uncontrollably. The air around them hummed with the charge of sexual excitement.

"Oh, my," she whispered, not looking at the scratches, but at him. Her breath quickened.

And his body tightened further, making his trousers damned uncomfortable. "Nothing you haven't seen before," he tried to quip, but his throat was suddenly parched, and his voice croaked.

"It was dark last time." She laid a hand on him, a warm, caressing hand, and his fingers convulsed on her hips. "Hunter, you're so beautiful."

He let out a sound, half laugh, half groan, then hissed when she swiped at the nasty scratches with the antiseptic. "That hurt worse than the damn thing did in the first place."

"I'm sorry." She pushed his shirt the rest of the way off his shoulders and continued to minister to him. "Hunter, about tonight—" She stopped and moistened her lips.

"What about it?"

"I . . . don't want it to be just a date."

"What do you want it to be?"

"More." Everything she felt swam in those eyes and quite suddenly, his heart skipped a beat. "So much more," she whispered.

Something close to panic overwhelmed him. He'd been down this road before, with women much more suited to him than the almost desperately wild Trisha Malloy. "I can't."

"Why? I might make a mess of things sometimes, and maybe drive you crazy once in a while, but I'd never demand things from you like your family does, I promise."

God, he didn't want to hurt her. But better now than later. "I've told you, it's not you. It's me. I—"

"If it's fear of getting hurt," she said in a hushed voice, "I'd never desert you at the altar. Or anytime, for that matter."

"I . . . just can't."

She glanced down at his lap. Confusion clouded her eyes as she obviously wondered why he couldn't, when his body seemed so willing. "It's not me you want?"

Unwanted tenderness washed over him. "It's not that simple, Trisha."

"Yes, it is. You either want me or you don't."

"You can see that I do," he said tightly.

"No," she denied. "I can see that you're hard, impressively so, by the way, but I don't know that it's for me."

He didn't want it to be for her. God, he didn't. The last thing he needed right now was to be betrayed by his own raging libido. "I've let things go on like this for too long. I should have said something before."

"About what?"

"I should have warned you," he said, wanting to kick himself. "Especially when we agreed to go out. But I can't . . . I don't . . ." Hell. "A date is all I can offer you," he said finally. "Anything more is out of the question."

"Why?"

Again, she glanced down at his hardness, clearly confused, and he wanted to groan and laugh at the same time. She thought he was telling her he couldn't have sex, but he was trying to tell her that a relationship was out of the question. He just didn't want to hurt her feelings.

"If you have problems," she said carefully, slowly, obviously measuring each and every word. "We'll get around it."

"No," he said. "We can't."

Her stubborn gaze met his. "Surely you can't think I'm out just for the physical aspect of a relationship. I'm vain, but not that vain, I hope."

He wanted to laugh, but this was too important. "It has nothing to do with that," he said. "I'm—" He glanced down at his tented trousers. "I'm functioning perfectly fine."

"Oh." Her cheeks flushed.

"Tonight was a mistake," he said gently. "I thought I could handle just the one date, but I can't."

"So take two." A sweet smile crossed her face. "Or three."

How was he supposed to resist her? "Trisha, this is difficult, the most difficult thing I've ever done, but—"

"No." Biting her lip, suddenly awkward, she set down the antiseptic bottle and backed away from him.

He rose, needing to explain, but she lifted a hand to ward him off. "How dense I am," she said with a little mirthless laugh. "You've been trying to explain this to me and I just keep missing the point."

"No," he said firmly. "It's my fault."

"Gallant to the end. Well, let me make it easier for you," she whispered. "I'll go. Excuse me." She ran from the room.

While he appreciated the great rear view of her biker

shorts as she left the room—and what they covered as well—it didn't tell him a thing about the woman. Or how badly he'd hurt her.

Rising, he followed her into her bedroom, where she paced with nervous energy. "Trisha?"

"I'm sorry." She whirled to face him, her hands clasped behind her back.

"You've already said that. It wasn't your fault."

"No, I mean I'm sorry for this." Before he realized what she was doing, she'd come forward, taken one of his hands in hers.

Something clicked and cold metal hit his wrist.

"I'm sorry," she said once more as he stared down at his wrist in utter surprise.

She'd handcuffed his left hand to the footboard of her bed.

THIRTEEN

"What the hell is this? A joke?" Hunter tugged at his caught wrist.

"No joke." Trisha rubbed nervous, damp palms down her thighs. She held up the key. "You're really handcuffed to my bed."

"Why?" He stared down in amazement, using his free hand to finger the steel that held him. "These are real."

A laugh escaped her. Carefully, she set the key down on her dresser, out of his reach. "Quite real," she said, looking at him. "And so are my feelings for you."

Oh, she had his complete attention now, and still shocked by what she'd done, he hadn't started to get angry yet, but she knew he would long before she was done.

But she had to tell him, had to do it now before he ran out of her life and never looked back. For as brave as this man was, he was terrified of the feelings that ran between them.

"Trisha—"

"I love you, Hunter Adams."

His eyes widened and he stepped toward her, jerking up short as the cuffs held him. "Dammit. Uncuff me, Trisha."

"I can't," she said softly. "Not until we talk."

"I wanted to talk last night, you wouldn't have anything to do with it. You don't have to cuff me for that."

"It's not me I want to talk about."

He sank to the bed and stared at her first, then at his captive wrist. "I can't believe this. I just can't."

Heart galloping in response to what she was about to do, Trisha slowly moved closer, keeping her eyes on his. "You can't believe a lot of things," she said, her voice shaking a little despite her best efforts to control it. "Mostly that my feelings for you are as real as yours are for me."

He looked a little panicked, but she knew it wasn't being restrained to the bed that caused it; it was her attempt to probe the feelings he'd rather keep to himself.

"I haven't misled you," he said. "I've been as honest as I can."

"There's the problem right there," she said softly, sinking to the bed beside him. "You're not being honest with yourself, so how can you be honest with me? You have feelings, deep feelings, though for some reason, you'd rather I think you cold." With light fingers, she reached out and touched the bunched muscle of his chest above a particularly nasty scratch. The muscle jerked and quivered. "But you're not cold at all," she whispered. "And neither are you immune to me. It hurts, Hunter. It hurts to watch you deny what's between us."

Anguished tension lined his face. "I hate knowing

I've hurt you." He tried to lift a hand to touch her, but was again thwarted by the handcuff. With a noise of frustration, he used his other hand, tracing a soft line over her cheek. "And I do . . . care for you. More than anyone, but—"

"No. No buts." She hushed him with a finger over his lips. "Do you have any idea how wonderful it feels to hear you say you care? Even when I do things that make you nuts, like smash myself into a tree on Rollerblades, you still care."

"Or when you weed-whack the sprinklers into pulp?"

She winced. "You knew about that?"

"Trisha," he said on a groaning laugh, lifting the cuffed hand. "What's this about?"

"It's about what's between us, and why you won't let it be."

And in that instant time stood still.

Trisha felt the heat shimmer through her. No, she thought, she couldn't be alone in this, and she wasn't. His hand, which had dropped to her waist, trembled. Pain swam in his emerald eyes.

He started to draw back, but she stopped him with a touch to his face. Her eyes begged something of him, something he couldn't, wouldn't give. God, he needed to run, hard and fast, but the damn handcuff . . . What the hell was she doing? "Trisha," he said tightly. "Let me go."

Her gaze sad and solemn, she shook her head. "I love you, Hunter," she said simply, and so sincerely he had to swallow hard.

"Why?" he asked hoarsely, dropping his forehead to hers as emotion swamped him. "I don't understand why."

"That's easy." Cupping his face in her hands, she made him look at her. "I love the way you care for people, even when you don't want to." Her voice warmed him, soothed him, even when he didn't want it to. "I love how you take care of your family even when they don't deserve it. I love the way you throw yourself into each and every little thing you do, whether you're fixing my floor, or jogging, or just reading. I love to watch you concentrate, Hunter, how you furrow your brow and your green eyes go all intense. I love the way you get mad at me and keep your cool at the same time—no matter what's happened, you're so calm. You'd never hurt me, Hunter."

He closed his eyes against her dark, dreamy ones.

"I feel safe with you," she said. Her voice drifted low, sexy as she lost herself in thought. "And I love that too.

"I love it when you kiss me. How you do it with that shattering, intense determination of yours, giving me everything you've got. It makes me lose myself, Hunter."

Now his eyes opened to see her watching him with that secret little smile that always drew a helpless smile of his own.

Her fingers sank into his hair as she maneuvered her scarcely clad body closer, gliding against him suggestively. "Mostly," she purred, "I love how you touch me. I love your strong, slow hands, your easy touch that makes me go wild."

She lightly rubbed the hard tips of her breasts over his chest.

He groaned helplessly and her gaze sharpened, steady on his, making him realize she hadn't been lost in thought after all. She knew exactly what she was saying and to whom.

And given the way she nestled her hips closer to him, nudging seductively, she knew exactly what it was doing to him.

"Please," she whispered so lightly he had to lean close to hear. "Please."

The arm he had around her waist tightened. "Please, what?" he asked hoarsely.

"Please, tell me you want me as badly as I want you."

He did, oh, how he did. "You can't seduce me," he said.

"Why not?"

Yeah, why the hell not? his body demanded. Beneath his hand, he felt the bare skin of her stomach, exposed between the crop top and biker shorts. It was warm, smooth, and flexed tight with need. As if she sensed his hesitation, she set her hands on his bare chest and gently, insistently, pressed him back to the bed.

"Wait," he gasped, struggling to remember he didn't want this.

"I can't." With hands to his shoulders, she pinned him down.

He fell back, sprawled across the bed, his cuffed hand outstretched above his head, as Trisha crawled slowly up his body, skimming her lush curves over every inch of him. He couldn't bite back his groan, or keep his free hand from gliding down her spine, cupping and gently squeezing her bottom, pressing her to the hot, aching part of him that begged for release.

Trisha's breath caught, then she smiled gently down at him, her eyes filled with such love and tenderness his throat clogged. She dipped her head, but instead of kissing him as he'd expected, she slowly trailed her lips over his jaw, his ear, down his throat to the base of his neck. Her tongue darted out and flirted with his skin.

Again he moaned, knowing he'd lost before she'd even started. That she'd pushed him to the limit and drawn him in. Never mind his good intentions of holding back so she wouldn't get hurt, it was too late to save her feelings, and it sure as hell was too late to save his. The temptation of what she offered—love and affection—was simply too much to refuse.

Knowing it was wrong, that he shouldn't, he drew her even closer, slowly rolling his hips to hers.

"Finally," she breathed against his mouth. "Hunter . . . tell me."

For a minute fear flashed through him, rendering him mute. Scared, he was so damned scared. Of her. Of himself. Of this. "I don't want to hurt you," he murmured even as he held her close with his one hand. "Please, don't make me hurt you."

"You won't," she whispered. "You can't. Love me, Hunter."

Her heart broke a little at the anguish on his beautiful face, at the mixture of desire and nervousness she saw in his eyes, and she almost gave in and offered to release him, but this was too important. If she failed, everything between them was over, but if she won . . . She eased down into the circle of his arm, fitting herself to him, then lifted her gaze to his.

"I love you," she whispered, raising a bent knee over his thigh, brushing lightly over his lap.

"It's not love," he maintained through gritted teeth. "It's physical need. I want you, Trisha, there's no doubt." His hips surged upward in proof. "I'm insane with the wanting. I've wanted you ever since I saw you that first day in black vinyl and that damn leopard-spotted top with plaster dust all over it." His eyes glazed with the memory. "My body is desperate to be sheathed inside you, but it's *lust*, Trisha. Just lust. If you still want me, then, God, *please*, take me now before you kill me. But nothing will change after we go up in flames in each other's arms. It'll still be just lust."

Liquid heat shimmered up her spine, making her weak. "Is that what we'll do?" she asked breathlessly. "Go up in flames?"

"Oh, yeah. And more."

"Show me," she begged softly, pressing close. "Show me."

"But—"

"This is happening because of me, Hunter. I won't regret this, I promise. I know what I'm doing."

"Do you?" he wondered out loud, his voice rough with emotion. "Well, Lord help us both, because I sure don't." Gently, he nudged her up a little so he could kiss her, and kiss her he did, long and slow and deep. It went on, erotic, tender, warm, and with just that kiss, he became the seducer, and she the seduced.

His hand moved slowly over her, easy and light, but she didn't want gentleness, not now. Irrational as it was, she wanted heat, speed, consuming passion. She wanted to erase the fear of his leaving her, which was silly, since he still lay cuffed to the bed. He was going nowhere. It didn't matter, the urgency couldn't be denied. With awkward fingers, she reared up and yanked off her top, tossing it behind her to the floor.

She lowered her hands to explore his warm, hard chest. He reached for her, and again encountered the barrier of the cuffs. With a muttered oath, he arched his hips against her. "Let me go," he demanded. "I want to touch you."

"Not yet." Hardly able to breathe, she straddled him, tore frantically at the fastening of his trousers.

"First this," she said as his free hand lifted up to cup a breast, his long, sure fingers brushing over the tip.

With him touching her like that, her fingers, still struggling to undress him, stumbled, and refused to function.

He had to help her, and between his one hand and her badly shaking ones, she finally managed to free him and slide his pants off. Standing, she stripped off the rest of her clothes, vibrantly aware of his watching her every movement.

"First I show you how much more than lust this is."

She moved close again, greedily touching his shoulders, his chest, down his tensed belly, her hair sweeping in her fingers' path as she bent low to her task, dabbling tiny, nipping kisses as she went.

He murmured her name on a ragged breath.

"I love you," she said, her heart breaking a little over the strained torment on his handsome face. "Let yourself love me back, Hunter."

"No," he whispered roughly, shaking his head back and forth. "Not love—*God!*" He let out on an explosive sigh and bucked when her lips slid over his belly to a lean hip. "Definitely n-*not* love," he managed tightly, arching his back with a strangled sound when she kissed her way across the top of his thigh. "Just . . . lust," he gasped.

"No." She continued her exquisite torturing of his damp, sleek skin with her mouth.

With his limited mobility, he caressed her breasts, molded their shape, alternately worshiping and teasing until her hips rocked against the bedding. He had no idea how much more of this he could stand. Her body seemed to be made for him, the creamy texture, the incredible shape, the sweet taste . . . he'd never wanted anyone so much. The force of his need scared the hell out of him, but what terrified him even more was the thought of stopping.

Yet stop he must, before he caved in completely. He was only a breath away from begging. "Lust," he whispered one more time, but she just shook her head and continued her trek over his body with her mouth. He was losing it, completely losing it. Her wild hair caressed his chest, his belly, his thighs, and his every muscle tensed. "Trisha," he whispered desperately, his will-power starting to break.

Gripping her head, he started to pull her up, desperate to taste her again, to kiss that full, sexy mouth, but she resisted, dragging her lips down his taut thighs. Then back up again, pausing at their apex. He felt her warm breath on him and he knew he'd die if she left him now.

"Oh, please," he groaned, his fingers entwining in her hair.

Her mouth, hot and wet, had him writhing against the constraint of the handcuffs. He'd never felt like this, never. Torment. Exhilaration. Control was out of the question. Tugging her up, he looked deep into her eyes, dizzy with arousal and confusion. "God, Trisha, what are you doing to me?"

Her smile was watery, and filled with such heart-wrenching love and warmth, his own eyes stung. "I'm making love to you," she whispered. "Do you like it?"

"No," he lied, his voice as harsh as his breathing. Closing his eyes so he couldn't see her delectable body didn't help. He could still feel her. "Uncuff me."

"I love you," she whispered again. "I'll never stop, you know. You can trust me."

"No."

"Then I'll just have to keep telling you," she said gently. "And showing you." Forcing the issue, she rose up and sank onto him with tantalizing slowness, taking him into her, one glorious inch at a time. "And showing, and showing . . ."

He moaned, grabbed her hip with his hand, but instead of pushing her away, he drove into her again, hard and deep.

Her cry of triumph washed over him. "I love you," she gasped, gripping his shoulders. "So much."

"Just don't stop," he entreated, then moaned low in his throat when she rocked her hips. His fingers touched her intimately, desperate to bring her to the same pitch of arousal he was at. Almost immediately her muscles clenched around him and she cried out, lost in her release. It was the most beautiful sight he'd ever seen, he thought, dazed, staring up at her. He'd never experienced anything like this. Blood pounded through his body, claimed his senses.

Her fingers dug into his chest as she braced herself on shaking arms and looked down at him, eyes glazed. "Your turn," she whispered.

No, he tried to say. *No.* "Yes," he said thickly, plunging into her once, twice, a third time. And despite his intentions, his body rejoiced. His emotions shattered. His heart opened, his wounded soul stirred, and as he burst into oblivion he heard himself call out her name, heard her own helpless response as she shuddered and came again.

When he could open his eyes, he realized Trisha lay collapsed in a damp heap on top of him, trembling. He

shook, too, though the slight weight of her soothed him
beyond belief. He went to wrap his arms around her.

And came up against the steel handcuffs.

At the clank of steel, Trisha stiffened, then rose off
him, studiously avoiding his gaze. Without a word, she
reached up and pressed the lever on the cuff. They
snapped open.

He'd never been locked in.

Before he could reach for her, she'd scooped up her
clothes and left the room.

"So much for your promise to never leave me,"
Hunter said lightly a minute later, when he found her
sitting in a tight ball on the porch bench.

She didn't answer.

It started low in his belly, the first stirring of an anger he rarely acknowledged. To calm himself, he looked
around.

Night had fallen, the full moon allowing him a good
view of her drawn face. But she didn't move, didn't look
at him, and he found himself simmering. "Do I need to
handcuff and seduce you to get you to talk?"

Her eyes closed. "I'm sorry."

The way she'd withdrawn into herself, when he
wanted—no, *needed*—answers only further angered him.
"Trisha, what the hell just happened?"

"I don't know."

"You don't know?" he asked, amazed. "You—" The
air whooshed out of his lungs. "You don't know."

She shook her head miserably, and though it rarely
happened, he did indeed lose his calm. "Dammit, you
sure as hell do! I'm beginning to see that you always
know exactly what you're doing, no matter how it looks.

Beneath that flighty, lackadaisical exterior lives a woman who knows *exactly* what she wants."

She flinched. "I deserved that."

Hunter, still stunned by what had been the most sensuous, erotic experience of his life, sank to the bench beside her. He felt so many things, he didn't know where to start, but his anger seemed as good a place as any. "You tied me to your bed to get your way," he said, still disbelieving.

"Not tied, exactly."

In spite of himself, he flushed. To be so caught up in the passion she had engendered in him . . . so enslaved to feelings that he never realized he could have freed himself—it mortified him. "I think I should be furious."

"Yes," she said dully. "You should."

Oh, he was angry, all right, but so much more as well. "Strange as this is to say since it's the least of my worries right now, all I can think is: How many men have you done that to?"

Her head jerked up in surprise as she at last looked at him. "Not that I expect you to believe me, but you're the first, Hunter."

"That's something, I suppose," he said with a sigh, looking down at his wrist and remembering what it had been like to be helplessly aroused when he didn't want to be . . . and how that very feeling had turned him on even more.

"I'm sorry," she whispered suddenly. "It was very wrong, and I'm so sorry." She hid her face in her hands. "I'm so embarrassed. I don't suppose you'll just go away?"

He laughed shortly. "You tied me up—or let me think I was tied up—seduced me until I was *begging* you, and now *you're* embarrassed?"

Her voice was muffled by her hands. "Can't we just forget it?"

He'd never forget it. "I doubt that." Each moment that passed saw him madder—at himself. He'd done this to himself, and now it had to stop. He couldn't let her go on feeling the way she thought she felt about him. Not when he wouldn't let himself return those feelings. To do so would be a big mistake.

Yet he couldn't stop himself from asking to hear it again, to watch her when she told him how she felt. Slowly, he turned her to him. "You said you loved me."

"I do."

So simple. So easy. So genuine, he wanted suddenly, inexplicably, to cry. His anger couldn't hold up in the face of this. "How—" He had to clear his throat. "How do you know?"

Unbearable sorrow stared at him from her dark eyes. "I just do."

Couldn't she see that wasn't enough? *"How?"* he demanded roughly. "How do you 'just know'?"

Her shoulders lifted helplessly. "Because you're never not in my thoughts. I think about you until I can't get anything else done, then I think about you some more. I see you and my heart starts pounding for no reason . . . until you look at me. Then I melt, just completely melt." She inhaled deeply and shook her head, as if amused at herself. "All you have to do is say my name and I get warm and shivery at the same time."

"It's lust," he whispered.

"No," she denied. "Lust is different from this. Lust is just the flesh." She lifted a hand to her chest. "Every part of me—my body, my heart, my soul—they all crave you, Hunter. It's never been like that for me before, and while that's scary, it just feels right. So very right. For the first time in my life I feel happy, sated, relaxed. And terrified."

He let his breath out slowly. "Well, I understand the terrified part pretty well."

She shrugged, her cheeks a little red, as if her admission had embarrassed her. "I guess you don't understand the rest."

"That's not true. I feel some of those things, I had just hoped it was a bad strain of the flu. Something that would pass." Though he had an unnerving suspicion that it wouldn't.

She let out a little laugh, then fell silent.

He wanted to do several things at once; wanted to throttle her and make her take back the words she'd said, the words he knew he'd never forget. Those three little words that had struck panic in his heart. He also, ridiculous as it seemed, wanted to get down on his knees and beg her to say them again, wanted to know those feelings weren't just a response to the physical attraction between them. Wanted to know she'd feel that way forever.

But most of all, he wanted to grab her and yank her close, and not let her go.

Did he love her?

Good Lord, how could he be thinking like this? Hadn't two fiancées taught him anything? He wasn't cut out for this. But damn Trisha for making him want what he couldn't have.

"How mad are you?"

"I have no idea," he said finally, then sighed. "You tried to force me to admit something I wasn't ready to admit. I told you before, I didn't want to hurt you, but—"

"I know," she said quickly. "You don't feel it back,

it's just lust. And it was wrong of me to try to prove you loved me." Leaping off the bench, she clasped her hands, avoided his gaze. "I gave you my word I'd never do that to you again, not that I expect you to believe it."

He stood up too. "I believe everything you say," he told her quite honestly.

"Why?"

When she looked at him like that, there was no way he could maintain any sort of righteous anger. Had no one ever trusted her before? Believed in her? Of course not, he thought, remembering how she'd grown up. "I believe you because you've never lied to me before. You've always been refreshingly honest, Trisha. It's one of the things I like most about you. I don't expect you to suddenly change your ways and start lying now."

"I see." She opened her front door, stepped inside.

"Trisha?"

Hesitating, she looked at him.

There was so much more they had to discuss. Her past and her fear of moving, for one. For he could never consider selling this place until he knew she'd be all right, and he *had* to sell. He knew that for certain now. Then there was the little matter of her thinking she was in love with him. He couldn't leave her knowing she thought that.

From his back pocket, he lifted the pair of now-harmless handcuffs, dangling them from his fingers. Safe in his front pocket was the key. "That was some first date."

Her face reddened. "Yes, well . . ."

The cuffs clanked noisily as he swung them. "I don't suppose you'd mind if I kept these as a souvenir."

"I didn't think you'd want any reminders."

Surprised, he looked at her. "It's not likely I'll forget it, with or without the cuffs."

She bit her lip and looked full of regret.

"Don't," he said softly. "I'm trying to tell you I don't want to forget tonight, any more than you do."

"Oh."

"I'll never forget making love to you," he told her, watching her eyes darken. "Never."

She smiled sadly and disappeared behind her door.

FOURTEEN

Two days. Two long, restless, nightmarish days.

Eating and sleeping had become a luxury Hunter's body didn't seem to want. His project and his NASA team had kept him busy in the lab for nearly forty-eight hours, starting the morning after his most interesting "date" with Trisha.

He'd not seen her since, staggering into bed late and rising far before the sun. And she'd not answered his many phone messages to her machine. When, out of worry, he called Leather and Lace, Celia answered, and told him in a kind but firm voice that Trisha was busy.

Not surprisingly, she hadn't returned his call.

There'd been no more disasters, no holes in the floors, no fires, no lipstick messages. And no beautiful woman sprawled out on her rear in Rollerblades, looking up at him with dark, laughing, mischievous eyes.

The handcuffs sat harmlessly on his dresser, making him wonder if it had all been a dream.

Some dream. He still couldn't think about that night

without his body reacting in the expected, uncomfortable manner.

God, he missed her. What made it even more unbearable was that he didn't want to. He tried, quite desperately, to keep his mind off her. And with his mission coming up, and so much left to do before they launched, it should have been easy.

Yet even as he led his team through the required prelaunch procedures and pored over his research data, some of his mind remained on that almost unbelievable evening he'd spent with Trisha. The way her hair had fallen over him, tickling his skin. How her lips had felt gliding lightly over every inch of him. How, despite her boldness, he'd known by her awkward, fumbling fingers that she'd never done anything like that before.

It was very difficult to continue feeling any sort of indignation over that night, but anger was all that kept him from admitting he might be wrong about the depth of his feelings for her.

He knew she thought she'd gambled on that night, and lost. It was why she'd made herself scarce. But Hunter was a man who liked to think everything through completely, and he liked to do this in his own time, in his own way. He'd done little but think, but he'd come to no definite conclusion—another troubling fact.

Since when could he not come to a definitive conclusion? Since when had things not been either black or white, but a muddled gray?

The fear in the pit of his belly didn't abate on the third day, and as he walked out of the lab late that night, he thought he just might be exhausted enough to fall into his bed and crash. He hoped.

The lot was nearly empty. He waved at the guard and walked toward his car, pulling out his keys. It had been the day from hell, where nothing had gone right, and everything that could go wrong had. Finally, after consuming an entire roll of antacid tablets, which Heidi had been kind enough to procure for him, he was forced to admit it: The overwhelming fear wouldn't go away until he faced it—and Trisha.

But doing that would make him think about his feelings for her, and those feelings went far deeper than he would have thought possible. In fact, he thought while inhaling a big gulp of air and even more antacids, it was quite possible he loved her every bit as much as she claimed to love him.

"You look as though you've been punched in the gut."

In the relative dark of the half-moon and deserted parking lot, Hunter jerked and turned.

"Sorry." Celia, with her spiked light green hair and rows of silver jewelry, waved and smiled at him, looking far from apologetic. "Didn't mean to startle you."

"Hmm," he said noncommittally, unlocking his car. "I suppose I should be surprised to see you, but somehow I'm not."

"There's that famous wit. The one that got you that reputation for, what is it they call you? Devil?" A wide grin flashed in the dark.

He hated that nickname. "Nasty job, cajoling money out of very wealthy, lonely women. But someone's got to do it."

"Ah, sarcasm." She nodded, her hair bobbing. "That's something I understand well. You hate your reputation, and I guess, given what I know about you, I can see why."

"What are you talking about?"

"It's not easy for you to have people get to know you, is it?"

Startled by her perceptiveness, he glanced at her. "Thought you sold panties. Didn't know you were a shrink as well."

Uninsulted, she laughed and slipped her hands into the back pockets of her bright red leather pants. "I'm a whole heck of a lot of things, Dr. Adams. But at the moment, mostly, I'm worried about my best friend."

That made two of them.

"What I want to know," she said, "is what are you going to do about it?"

Tossing his briefcase into the car, he straightened and sighed. "Not that it's any of your business, but I've been working night and day."

"Hmmph."

He felt like a six-year-old, duly chastised. "I've been trying to call her."

The dark look she shot him told him what he already knew—*not good enough*.

"Do you have any idea what she's doing at this very minute?" Celia asked.

He'd thought he'd been in a state of real fear for the last few days, but it was nothing compared with the terror that gripped him now. "God, what has she done?"

Celia laughed, but sobered quickly. "I should let you find out the hard way, I really should. But, well, she . . ."

"She what?" he asked in an ominous voice that none of the entire ten thousand employees of the lab would have been able to ignore. "Just tell me."

"She's moving out. Tonight."

❖━━━━━━━❖

Hunter completed the normally ten-minute drive in less than four. Taking the stairs to Trisha's apartment three at a time, he debated for maybe a millisecond about knocking. Then forsook the niceties and stormed in.

She sat on the couch, a faraway expression on her face as she stroked Duff in her lap. Immediately he saw her surrounded by a sea of empty boxes.

His sigh of relief sounded loud in the silent room. "I caught you in time, then," he said, sticking his hands in his pockets to keep them off her.

Her gaze leaped to his, though she didn't move a muscle. "I didn't hear you knock."

"That's because I didn't." She sounded distant, cool, and so damn familiar he wanted to draw her up and gather her close. Instead, he stepped into the room and leaned against the wall. "What's going on, Trisha?"

Her eyes drank in the sight of him, and he knew what she saw. Ruffled hair, haphazardly knotted tie, haggard features. Work. Too much work, that's all that was wrong with him.

This insane panic at the sight of the moving boxes was all due to too much work.

Oh, like hell. Lying was impossible, especially to himself. In two strides, he was standing in front of her; then, ignoring her startled squeak of surprise, he hauled her up, wrapped her in his arms, and looked at her.

Her voice, when she spoke, was shaking. "Hunter—"

He kissed her, thoroughly. Ah, this, *this* was what he'd wanted, needed, craved beyond belief all week, and he buried his face in her neck, pressing her close. Dragging his lips over her soft skin, he listened to her ragged breathing. As his hands slid over her, pulling her closer still, a little sound of pleasure rose from her throat and she fisted her hands in his hair to bring his face back to hers.

The kiss consumed him.

He lost himself in it, in the feel of her against him. "Trisha," he groaned, and took her mouth again.

Then she shoved him away, hard.

Chest heaving, she stared at him. He stared back, aroused, stunned, terrified all at once.

"Is this some more of that lust we talked about?" she demanded.

No. God, no. "Yes."

"Go away," she whispered, putting a trembling hand to her chest.

That little vulnerable gesture tore at him. "I can't."

"You've managed well enough these past few days." With a suspicious sheen to her eyes, she turned away and knelt before a box.

"I needed to think." That sounded lame, even to his own ears. "Trisha, I—"

"I needed to think too," she said quietly. "And this is best—for both of us, I think."

Suddenly he knew exactly how she'd felt the other night when she'd had a panic attack. His windpipe tightened, cutting off his air. "Moving? That's the answer?"

She nodded and reached for the closest bookshelf at her side. Grabbing a handful of books, she tossed them into the box. Blindly, since her scalding tears didn't allow for much vision, she grabbed another handful, blinking frantically to hold back the flow.

"Trisha."

Lord, that voice. He dropped to his knees beside her, silently took the books from her hands, and set them aside. Turning back, he touched her shoulders until she looked at him. "I don't want you to move because of me."

She waited, but he said nothing else. No vow of love, or even undying lust. Nothing that gave away one iota of feeling, except for the torment shining in his deep green eyes. So he hadn't gotten over his fear yet, damn him. She loved him, more than her own life, but what else could she do? "I'm not moving for you," she managed. "I'm doing it for me."

He grimaced. "You wouldn't have considered moving before I came here."

"Maybe not." She tried to twist free, but he held her with a gentle yet firm grip. "I'm going to do this, Hunter." Her heart sent up a protest, which she ruthlessly squelched. Instead she surveyed her beautiful wide-open apartment.

Much as she loved it, it was nothing compared with being near the man she had come to love beyond reason. The man who had such a fear of letting go, of being hurt, that he couldn't allow himself to love her back.

"I can't stay here," she said quietly, swallowing her sob. "I'll find another home."

"Because of me?" Something flickered in his eyes. "You're leaving the only real home you've ever had, because of *me*?"

"Yes," she whispered. "You know I can't stay, feeling the way I do."

He took a deep breath, straightened his already impossibly straight shoulders. "I got a call today from the realtor. He found a buyer."

No, she wouldn't cry. "I see. That's nice for you."

His voice, when it ended the pained silence, sounded husky with emotion. "They intend to rent the place out, not live here. So I put a clause in the contract about your staying."

Her entire body went rigid. "Oh." Her fingernails dug painfully into her palms, holding the tears at bay. "That was thoughtful of you."

His shoulders hunched, and since he already towered over her, she felt surrounded by him. "I don't want you to leave because of me," he said again very softly. He bent his head close to hers, rubbing his slightly rough cheek over her smooth one.

Guilt. It drove him in a way she understood all too well. Her aunt had been the queen of guilt, but Trisha had vowed not to be controlled by her emotions any longer. "You can't always have your way, Hunter."

"Maybe not," he admitted. "But I'm going to have my way in this. This place means everything to you and I won't take it from you." His voice, sure and steady, cracked. "And I won't let you take it from yourself either."

"I'm leaving," she insisted, hardening herself to his anguish. "You can't afford for me to stay. I'll probably destroy something else by accident. Maybe the roof this time. I don't know how, and I certainly won't mean it, but it'll just happen."

"I don't care—"

"I'm ready to move on anyway."

He stood and reached for her hand, which she refused, pushing to her feet by herself. "Thought I'd try something completely different," she said with a light shrug. "Maybe go on a long vacation first, to Tahiti or somewhere."

He frowned. "By yourself?"

"Yeah." She forced a smile past her aching heart.

"Meet some new people. Then maybe a cruise to Alaska. Check out some glaciers."

He looked horrified. "Glaciers?"

"Why not? I need a challenge."

"Trisha," he said slowly, "with your track record, I don't think glaciers are a good idea."

Oh, anger helped, it really did. "Despite what you think, I can handle myself."

"I know," he said with a sad smile. "And you're quite good at it. You've had to be, with no one else to do the job."

The tenderness in his gaze made her yearn and ache even more. "You have no right to do this," she whispered. "No right at all."

"Do what?"

"Be so . . . kind. Caring. I want to hate you, Hunter. Please, let me."

His sad smile broke her heart. "You know, we never had our little talk."

"About?" She crossed her arms defensively, knowing damn well what.

"Remember that night you had your panic attack? I had some questions for you then, but you've managed to avoid me ever since."

"*I've* avoided *you*?" she asked incredulously, and laughed.

"That's right," he said evenly. "You're fine, as long as we're talking about anything but yourself, your past."

She hugged her arms closer to herself and wondered how they'd gotten to this point. "My past has nothing to do with the here and now."

"Hmmph," he said in obvious disagreement. Bending, he began to collapse the empty boxes with a quick efficiency. "Tahiti," he muttered.

"Don't fold up those boxes. I need them."

He ignored her. "Know what I think?" he asked casually, folding yet another moving box. "I think you use this slightly wacky, wild-woman thing as a shield. I think it's an effort for you to push yourself to live life to its fullest, because you never got the chance before."

His hands stilled. His gaze met hers, held it. "Isn't that right?" he asked softly.

Her only defense was sarcasm, and she usually used it well. "That would suit you just fine, wouldn't it? If I was really someone else. But if you're hoping that beneath this crazy facade lives a calm, elegant, and sophisticated woman, you're sorely mistaken."

"Of course I'm not."

"Really?" She let out a little laugh. "Tell me something. You like everything about me, every little thing?"

"Well . . ." His lips twitched. "Everything but the window rattling. If you'd just turn down the music, just a little bit . . ."

"Stop it," she said quietly, not feeling like bantering. "I'm not your type, you've said that often enough. Don't tease me about it."

"Oh, you're my type," he said silkily. "I'm just not yours." In the center of a sea of boxes, he turned around and lifted his hands. "Trisha, I'm not good at this, at keeping a woman happy for long. I've told you, I don't want to hurt you."

Too late for that. Much too late. But with Hunter looking at her, his eyes gentle and regretful, she couldn't tell him so.

"Don't move out of here," he said suddenly, standing and touching her face. "Please, I'll leave, but not you. You belong here, and I want to be able to picture you, happy in your home."

He'd leave. He'd leave so she could stay. Some compromise, her heart cried, but what choice did she have?

"Please," he whispered, dropping his hand from her. "Promise you'll stay."

"You're still going to sell."

It wasn't a question, but he answered her with a curt nod. "Yes."

Locking her knees together, she lifted her chin, prepared to be curt in return. But one look at him and the words dried up in her mouth. His expression, so carefully blank, told her he purposely, desperately hid his thoughts. Only the searing, tortured glaze in his eyes gave him away as he waited for her answer.

Everyone in his life left him or took from him. No one stayed of their own accord, just for him.

She'd be the first.

"Maybe I will stay a little longer," she said slowly, heart thumping as she hoped to ease him somehow.

It worked. His body relaxed, the tension drained instantly, or most of it. There was still some left in his gaze as he looked at her for one long telling moment before turning and quietly walking out of her life.

The next day Trisha took a phone call from Sam Walters, the realtor. The minute he said his name, she couldn't help but picture a little weasel, sniffing and chortling over the prospect of a huge sale. Gritting her teeth, she suffered the banalities of casual conversation until he got to the point of his call.

Thrilled at the imminent sale, he simply wanted to assure her that the prospective new owners did indeed want her to stay on as a tenant. And as *the previous owner* had stipulated in no uncertain terms, she would be allowed to transfer her current lease.

It seemed Hunter had been busy.

The offer far surpassed her hopes, she had to admit as she hung up the phone. But that's not why she suddenly dropped her head to her desk and began to sob with helpless abandon.

No, it was the realtor's parting words that threatened to shred apart her heart.

On top of allowing her to stay in her place for as long as she wished, the "previous owner" had taken care of one more thing.

Hunter Adams had done what he seemed to do best—taken care of those he felt responsible for. It was apparently the only way he had of showing his true feelings.

It certainly was the only evidence she had of how much he cared for her, but she'd take it and hold it dear to her heart nonetheless, knowing that for Hunter, it was a profound expression of his feelings, the most she was likely ever to receive.

He'd settled her rent with the new owners for the next five years.

FIFTEEN

She dreamed of Hunter that night, dreamed of his fathomless green eyes, of his sweet, yet wicked smile, of the intensity that always simmered just beneath his surface.

She dreamed of his incredible mouth on hers, soft at first, then more seductive. Her body reacted, arched up against the bedding . . . and came in contact with a warm, hard, strong body.

"It's me," he said in a husky whisper, startling her fully awake.

Hunter.

In the silvery light she saw his face, saw the tense lines of fear and need warring with good sense.

"I'm sorry if I scared you," he said softly.

He wore only a T-shirt and sweatpants. Kneeling by the bed, he leaned close and dipped his mouth to the frantically racing pulse at the base of her neck, then groaned at his first taste of her. "God, Trisha, don't . . . I don't think I can stand it if you . . . Please, don't make me go."

As if she could.

"Trisha?"

In answer, she moved back and made room. He lay down in the warm space, half covering her body with his own, the blankets still between them. His powerful arms shook slightly as he drew her to him.

"I dreamed you were gone," he whispered raggedly. "I had to come make sure."

"I thought *you* were gone."

In her arms, he shivered, though he felt warm to the touch. "I tried to go." He pulled her tighter. "Couldn't."

He expected her to leave him. He'd been waiting for it, so sure he would be left once again. In fact, he'd done everything in his power to chase her away, to ensure that she would go. Well, she thought with a deep breath, this test was about to come to an end.

"I'm here," she whispered, wrapping her arms around him. "I'm right here."

"I can't stop thinking of you . . . of what you do to me." He untied his sweats and drew her hand inside to his very solid erection. "I need you, Trisha. So much." He moaned when she stroked him. "God. Please."

She murmured, knowing she could no more refuse him than stop breathing. With a sigh of relief, he stripped off his shirt, pulled the covers back from between them. At the sight of her, he let out a strangled breath.

She was naked.

"I didn't finish my laundry," she said inanely, thinking she needed to explain why she'd chosen to sleep in the buff. "And—"

"You're so beautiful." His hands cupped the soft curves of her breasts, a sound of pure male satisfaction coming from deep in his throat when he found the tips hard and pebbly. "Last time you took care of me." His lips kissed their way over her collarbone. "This time it's for you. All for you."

She wanted to deny that, wanted it to be for him, too, but then his lips replaced his fingers, slowly surrounding her breasts, and she couldn't speak at all, much less think.

His talented fingers didn't stay idle, but worked their way down her belly with featherlight strokes, making her shiver with anticipation. "Hunter . . ."

"Shhh," he murmured against her skin. "Just feel."

Then he drew her nipple hard into his mouth at the same instant as he slipped a finger inside her, and she had to bite back her scream, writhing against the bed.

"No." Lifting his head, he whispered roughly, "Don't hold back, Trisha. I want it all." Then he tugged rhythmically on her with his mouth, his fingers matching the motions below.

Arching back, she fisted her hands in the sheets. The sharp, searing need stunned her. It rained over her in waves, and she knew it wasn't just her, that Hunter felt it too. He trembled with it.

"Let go," he whispered again, his thumb brushing against the very core of her.

Utterly incapable of fighting it any longer, she let herself go with a soft cry he immediately swallowed with his mouth.

"Yes," he whispered triumphantly, shifting lower, lower, then lower still. His hands were everywhere. His teeth nipped her inner thigh, and she squirmed and pushed to get closer, to rush him, to ease the insane renewed need. He just held her down gently with his arms, then splayed her legs wide, his nimble, deft tongue tracing over her knowingly.

"Hunter." It was all she could manage, and even then, it came out more like a muffled sob. He explored her slowly, relentlessly, with a thoroughness that left her gasping, each nerve and muscle clenched tight, trembling, waiting, wanting. So close, so desperately close.

Then he stopped.

"Not yet," he panted, rearing up to shuck his sweats. "I want to be inside you when you come again." He shuddered as he came back to her, his hips moving rhythmically.

With torturous slowness, he sank into her. Steel into wet velvet, and she rocked against him, desperate now for more.

"Don't move," he gasped, dropping his forehead to hers, gripping her hips to hold her still. "I want—*slow*. I want this to last. God, don't move . . . I can't—"

"Hunter," she cried out, lifting her hips. She couldn't keep still, tried but just couldn't. That she'd reduced this strong man to a trembling mass of muscle empowered her. Moving against him, she sucked in her breath at the surge of dangerous heat, the unleashed hunger. "Now, please, now."

His control was slipping, she knew that by the fierce concentration on his face. She strove to shatter the rest and took his mouth with hers.

He groaned, but still didn't move.

She expected the slap of fear, knew it stemmed from the strength of her love for him, from her knowledge that he wouldn't allow himself to return that love.

She just didn't expect him to feel the fear too.

He went stiff in her arms, his face drawn and tormented. "No," he said hoarsely, levering himself up. "I shouldn't have come. Dammit, I shouldn't have come."

Her fear was nothing compared with his, she thought

with a burst of raw emotion that stung her eyes. "Yes, you should have. I'm right here, Hunter. Love me."

His eyes, shimmering with a bleak despair, met hers.

He was going to refuse, and she couldn't allow it. Lifting her legs around his waist, she pulled him back to her, met his mouth for a long, drugging, fervent kiss. "I'm right here," she whispered again, clutching his wide, damp shoulders. "I'm right here."

With a groan, he scooped her close and whispered her name hoarsely, driving himself into her, shattering them both as they shared a drenching, volcanic climax.

She awoke to a blaring alarm clock, the bright sun, and the noisy chirping of birds.

Jerking upright, Trisha stared at her room, trying to get her bearings. She was alone, and if it hadn't been for the sweet ache between her thighs, she might have thought she'd dreamed the entire night.

She might as well have, for all the good it would do her. Obviously, Hunter Adams had decided she wasn't worth the possible pain, and she had only herself to blame if her heart broke now.

On the other side of her room, her alarm still blared, and given that it was nearly ten o'clock, she had to assume the thing had been blaring for nearly three hours.

How could she have slept that way?

Easy—exhaustion, mental and physical.

Her quick shower didn't help much, nor did Celia's amused, knowing glance when Trisha dashed into the store, hours late.

"You had a delivery this morning," Celia said casually. "It's on your desk."

Trisha nodded reluctantly, wondering what crazy

shipment she'd received today. Without much energy, she moved toward her office.

She'd tried to prepare herself for the realization that Hunter couldn't handle love, but she hadn't been successful. It still hurt. But the truth remained; no matter how patient she was, he just wouldn't allow himself to feel.

She told herself it was okay to grieve, but that she had to move on. Had to, or she'd never get over it. She'd been hurt before, by people who *did* claim to love her, so this shouldn't have come as such a big surprise.

What did come as a surprise was the single red rose on her desk with the card that simply read, *The house is not for sale.*

Trisha stared at the card with hands that suddenly didn't seem steady. What did this mean? Obviously, Hunter had turned down the offer, taken the house off the market.

But why?

For once, Trisha's mind strayed far from the store as she worked. Would he come to her bed tonight?

If he did, would she let him?

She thought of the tortured glaze to his eyes, of the tension in his glorious body, of the aching emotion in his voice, and knew she would. The ravenous, dark hunger they shared for each other, the way he wrung things from her no one else ever had . . . Oh, yes. She'd have him again if he wanted. She'd do anything to ease his anguish.

Though it was the night when she and Celia always went out for dinner and a movie, Celia sent her home, saying she looked like she needed sleep.

Trisha needed something all right, only it wasn't sleep.

Walking up her stairs, she paused with a frown when she found her front door locked. She *never* locked it, and not because she didn't care about her apartment. She left it open because she could so rarely find her key.

It couldn't have been a burglar. One, she had nothing of value to take, and two, what kind of a thief locked up after himself?

It took her more than a minute to locate the nearly forgotten key in her huge, overstuffed purse. Then, still frowning, she unlocked the door and stepped inside.

Silence. Slightly messy, just as she had left it.

Duff sat on the couch, waiting, and she sighed, her body relaxing. "Hi, sweetie. It's so nice to have you here when I get home." She dumped her purse and sank down next to him. He crawled onto her lap with a low purr, rubbed his face against her, then settled down for a petting.

"You love me," she whispered, choking up. "It's enough for me. It is."

She hunched over him, hugging him close, soaking in the unconditional love that only an animal can provide. "Thanks." She smiled. "This self-pity thing really has to go. I'm fine. My life is fine."

Yeah. Everything was just peachy.

Then she heard it. A small, unidentifiable noise from down the hall that made her freeze.

With Duff right there on the couch next to her, there was no reason for a noise, and she remained tense on the couch for a long moment. Finally, she shrugged lightly, stroking the sleek cat. "Oh, Duff." She laughed. "My nerves are shot."

But a minute later she heard the noise again—the

distinct sound of her bedsprings. She stiffened, glancing at Duff, who merely licked his chops and proceeded to wash his face.

With a snort of disgust for her feline watchdog, she slowly rose, listening. Nothing.

Duff didn't so much as raise a single hair.

Just her overworked imagination, that's all.

Shrugging out of the blazer she wore, she stretched, then shivered. The early evening had gotten chilly, and her sleeveless lace shell wasn't nearly warm enough. Sweats, she decided. Glamourless, baggy sweats, and a big bowl of popcorn. No, make that chocolate, and lots of it.

But she came to a dead stop in the doorway of her bedroom, speechless.

Sprawled across her bed, wearing nothing but a lazy grin and her handcuffs, lay Hunter.

SIXTEEN

"Oh, my."

His grin widened.

"I—I thought you were at work."

"Nope." With a lift of his wrist, he showed her the handcuff, which he'd used to cuff himself to her headboard. "No work. As you can see, I'm . . . rather tied up at the moment."

Trisha, eyes wide, drank in the sight of Hunter's long, powerful body tied to the bed by his own will. Gloriously, magnificently nude. It was incredible, *he* was incredible. But what really caught her eye was the look in his. The calm, controlled certainty was back in those green depths, and added in was what she'd been waiting so long to see.

He winked.

Her knees wobbled. "Oh, my," she said again.

He laughed. *Laughed.* To Trisha, it was the sweetest sound she'd ever heard. The fist that had clenched tight around her heart slowly loosened.

"Hunter," she said quite steadily, in complete disregard of the pattering of her heart. "Not that you don't look quite splendid . . ." She ran her eyes down the length of him. "But *what are you doing*?"

"Catching a cold." His eyes shone with a teasing amusement, and much, much more. "Come here, Trisha."

Again, her gaze ran over him, stretched out so comfortably, so relaxed, so . . . ready, willing, and able. *Very* able, she thought as her breath stammered in her throat.

Her knees touched the bed without her having any conscious memory of walking across the room. Hunter watched, his gaze searing and laughing and needy all at the same time. It reminded her of Duff suddenly, and how he always sprawled on his back when he wanted his belly rubbed. But the man sprawled out before her had the sleek, powerful body of a cougar, not a housecat. Still, she laughed.

"Anybody ever tell you that you could seriously damage a man's ego if you stare at him and laugh?" Hunter asked conversationally, not looking insulted in the least. "Especially when he's in the altogether."

"I'm sorry." But she giggled again. "I didn't quite have this in mind when you took the cuffs."

"I know." He reached up and grasped one of her hands with his free one. "I wanted to surprise you."

"Well, you did that."

"Trisha, I'm sorry."

"For tying yourself to my bed?"

"No. For hurting you."

Her amusement drained. "You didn't do it on purpose."

"No," he agreed solemnly. "I didn't. But it doesn't change the fact that I withdrew when you needed me, refused to give you what I should have given from the beginning."

"Give me what?"

"My heart."

"Oh. *That*." She shrugged as if it didn't matter, but of course it did. And his words touched her deeply. "You've done what you could."

"No." He swallowed and stared at her ceiling. "Even now you're willing to think the best of me. Do you have any idea how humbling that is? Especially since I don't deserve it." With a deep breath, he met her gaze again. "I never gave you the same courtesy, Trisha. And all along, you thought that was because I didn't feel anything for you. But I did, I *do*, I was just a coward."

"Well . . ." She shrugged. "I am a little different. Compared to what you're used to—"

"No," he said in a harsh voice laced with soft tenderness. "Don't defend me, it was unforgivable. Doubting you, doubting us . . ." His voice dropped to a whisper. "I haven't been fair. I've purposely held back from you, while you gave me everything you had."

She stared unblinking at their linked fingers. "Why are you telling me this now?" she whispered, afraid to hope, unable to hold it back.

He brought her knuckles to his mouth, kissed her gently. "I can't do it anymore, Trisha. I've been lying to myself all along, telling myself I could control this, but I couldn't. It terrified me, to feel so open, so . . . exposed."

"It was the handcuffs," she whispered. "I'm sorry."

"Maybe." He let out a little laugh. "Somehow you made me feel even more vulnerable, stripped of every ounce of control and all inhibitions." He laughed again. "But God, it was good."

"So you decided to come back for seconds." She nodded to the cuffs.

"I thought maybe this would show how seriously I intended to fix the problem." He shrugged, an eloquent smile playing about his lips. "The key is on top of your dresser. I'm not going anywhere now, unless you let me go."

Helplessly, she smiled back. "What if I never do?"

His smile was slow and devastating. "I was hoping you wouldn't."

Was he offering her everything she'd ever wanted? "Why? What has changed?"

"Time. The constant nightmares of your leaving. Waking up alone in the mornings, when I knew I could have had you in my arms. Coming home at night and wishing you were there, waiting for me, blaring music and all."

"I was," she said quietly. "Waiting for you."

"I was afraid," he admitted. "So deathly afraid you'd turn me away. I'd done it to you often enough."

Self-conscious for some strange reason, considering that it was Hunter who was naked, she pulled her hand free and crossed her arms over her chest.

"Are you all right?" he asked softly, gazing up at her. "After last night—"

"So I didn't dream it," she said a little breathlessly. "I wondered, when I woke up and found you gone."

"You don't wake up easily in the morning," he said. "When I said we had to get up for work, you mumbled something about my early demise if I wouldn't be quiet and go away."

Vaguely she remembered grumbling at the big, warm hand that had tried to gently shake her into awareness. "I was tired."

"You haven't been sleeping well either, I suppose. God, I'm so sorry, Trisha."

So fast that it startled a gasp from her, his free wrist snagged hers, and tugged. She fell on him, her hair curtaining his face. Propping herself up on his chest with her elbows, she stared down at him, very aware of his sinewy body stretched beneath hers.

"Say you forgive me," he beseeched, running his free hand slowly down the delicate bones of her spine.

His touch made her shiver. "For what?"

"For being so slow and dim-witted that I fought this—" He broke off to kiss her until she was dazed.

But still he offered no word about what this all meant, if the flicker of hope and joy in her heart would be extinguished or stoked. "Hunter," she said slowly, her insides starting to turn to jelly from the sizzling heat they generated between them. "Maybe I'm a little slow, but couldn't you have just told me you're sorry for hurting me and left it at that?" Unable to keep the hurt from her voice, she went on, "Did you have to"—she bit her lip—"tease me? Remind me—"

"Remind you of what's between us?" he finished gently, cradling her face with his one free hand. "Yes, I *had* to. I wanted you to have it all in your head when I told you for the first time."

Her heart stopped. "Told me what?"

"How I love you with all my stubborn, cautious heart." He smiled again. "How I'll love you with that same unbending, rigid organ for the rest of my days."

"Oh," she exclaimed, her bones dissolving at the words she'd waited so long to hear. Suddenly weak, she dropped her forehead to his chest, her eyes filling with joyous, scalding tears.

"Trisha," he whispered, his own eyes misting as he

watched her. He lifted her face. "Please, don't cry. Anything but that. Throw something at me, smother me with your pillow, just don't cry."

The sob escaped her before she could control it, and his face twisted in a grimace. For the first time, he reached for her with both hands, then swore when he remembered the cuffs. "I'm too late, then," he said flatly, mistaking her tears, his face pale as the white sheet beneath him. "I'm so sorry I hurt you, I—"

Startled out of her joy, she stared at him. "You think I—" Gulping, she sat up next to him and swiped at her wet cheeks with the back of her hand. Then she laughed. "You love me." She laughed again. "You silly man. *You love me.*"

Reaching up, his thumb carefully wiped at a lingering tear. "Does it always make you cry when someone says that?"

"This is the first time I've ever heard it," she said, smiling from ear to ear. "And I'm not crying because I'm sad or hurt. These are happy tears." Unable to contain her pleasure and joy, she surged off the bed, dancing back a step when he reached for her.

"Come here," he demanded, smiling helplessly when she giggled and shook her head. "What are you doing— oh, my God."

She'd whipped off her top. The love swelling her heart made her giddy, intoxicated. With a wicked smile, she palmed the key from the dresser, slipped out of her shoes, then her skirt, laughing a little breathlessly when he murmured another heartfelt oath at his inability to reach her. "Your own fault," she whispered as she slid off her stockings and underwear. She lay down on the bed, snuggling close when he wrapped his arm around her.

He yelped when she pressed her cold feet to his, then

moaned when her quickly warming body slid against him.

"I'm so glad," she whispered, kissing his throat.

He rubbed his cheek to hers. "That I love you?"

"That you're just stubborn, not completely out of control. I'd hate to think you'd compromise yourself this way for just a date."

She reached up to free his hand, then squeaked in surprise when his hand came free of its own accord. "What—"

"I never clicked them closed." He grinned, a light, carefree grin she'd never seen before. "I wasn't sure you'd have mercy on me."

"You weren't crying for mercy last time," she reminded him, gasping when a hand slid down her spine, cupped her bottom. His fingers stayed, dallied until she gasped his name. Slowly, those fingers slid back up.

"Mercy," he whispered. "God, I love you."

She sighed as both his strong arms came around her. "I love you back, Hunter."

"I was counting on that," he said, the nerves back in his velvety voice. He looked at her, his usual composure and confidence gone. "Trisha."

Smiling, she lifted a shoulder. "What?"

"It took me a while to figure this all out, but as stubborn as I am, it's for keeps."

"What—what is?"

Lifting the fist he'd just freed, he turned it over, showing her his palm.

In its big center sat a huge diamond ring.

"When I look at you, I see my future," he said softly. He kissed her long and tenderly. "When I touch you, I know peace, the first I've had in a long time, if ever. You make me whole, Trisha."

"You do the same for me," she managed, her gaze glued to the most beautiful ring she'd ever seen.

"Then will you marry me, and make me whole for the rest of our lives?"

"Oh, my."

He smiled and took her hand. "I sure hope that's a prelude to yes, because I don't think I'll make it without you."

Her eyes filled and ran over as she stared at him dreamily, picturing their children running around the house, all replicas of their daddy, with his expressive green eyes, his capacity to love, his understanding.

"You have to say yes," he said a little urgently, clearly taking her silence for hesitation. "Who else will help me turn this duplex into the home it was meant to be?"

"I'll marry you," she said with a laugh. "Because I love you with everything I have. But as far as turning this house into a home . . ." She took a breath and plunged. "I might have given you just a little head start on that one. You see, I had this *little* accident today with the roof. But it's no problem. All you have to do is—"

His bark of laughter drowned out her next words.

THE EDITORS' CORNER

Since time began, women have struggled to be respected in the workplace. No longer damsels in distress, women have soared to the tops of their professions. Strength is measured in endurance, and with our own fifteenth anniversary coming this summer, we are celebrating strong women everywhere. Yet for all that our four heroines this month have accomplished, they learn that leaning on someone else for a change doesn't necessarily mean weakness. Relish these women in power and watch how their control crumbles in the wake of these fabulous heroes.

Helen Mittermeyer concludes her latest trilogy with the long-awaited **DESTINY SMITH,** LOVE-SWEPT #886, which is set once again in beautiful Yokapa County, New York. Helen visits with familiar friends and family as she reintroduces Destiny Smith and her soon-to-be-ex–husband Brace Coolidge.

When Brace refuses to sign the divorce papers and claims he wants to help adopt the two children Destiny has taken under her wing, she has no alternative but to come to an uneasy truce with the brash executive. With threats from all quarters hovering over their lives, Destiny and Brace struggle together to create a loving family for two children who have never known love. And in this struggle, can the two lovers find their way back to each other? Helen weaves a tale of turbulent emotion and sweet sensuality that brings together a rebel and the charming rogue who will try to tempt her into yielding her heart a second time around.

LOVESWEPT newcomer Caragh O'Brien presents her second release, **NORTH STAR RISING**, LOVESWEPT #887. Though river guide Amy Larkspur feels awkward in the bridesmaid dress she's wearing for her best friend's wedding, she doesn't show it when Josh Kita spies her on the balcony like a modern-day Juliet. The handsome widower knows that Amy's the *one*, whether he's ready for her or not. But with two young daughters to take care of, finding time to spend with Amy can get pretty hectic. Nevertheless, Josh pursues his beautiful dreamer with everything he's got. Amy can barely handle dealing with Josh, but add two children into the fold and she's definitely out of her league. Caragh O'Brien tries to solve the eternal puzzle of attraction in a novel as delightfully unpredictable as its spirited heroine.

In **JADE'S GAMBLE**, LOVESWEPT #888, Patricia Olney gives us Jade O'Donnell, single mother and co-owner of the Cinnamon Girl bakery, and Trace Banyon, sexy ex-fireman. Jade has had her share of marital strife—granted, it was only for half an hour, but it was enough heartache to last a lifetime. As a firefighter, Trace couldn't stop a mother and her son from dying, and in Jade and her son, Lucas, he sees his chance to atone for his past. Desperate to keep custody of Lucas, Jade is searching for a suitable candidate to be her husband. When Trace offers to step in, Jade decides that he's her only hope. United by a marriage of convenience, Jade and Trace soon learn that living as man and wife is a bigger gamble than they thought! Patricia Olney bakes up a savory romance to be tasted only by those who can handle happy endings.

Clint McCade teaches a few lessons in **BODY LANGUAGE** to chief executive officer Cassandra Kirk in Suzanne Brockmann's LOVESWEPT #889. World-renowned cameraman McCade has decided that his real home is with his best friend and true love, Sandy. The only problem is, she's in love with someone else. But like the pal that he is, McCade offers to help her get her man. Sandy is never surprised when McCade roars into town on the back of his Harley, but this time something's different. For one thing, McCade's never picked out her clothes or offered makeup advice before. And what is with those funny looks he keeps giving her, anyway? As the two begin a charade that becomes too hot for them to handle, they discover that the warm fuzzy feelings they have aren't just of friendship, but of love. Suzanne Brockmann proves her talent once again when she shows us the true meaning of best friends forever!

Happy reading!

With warmest wishes,

Susann Brailey *Joy Abella*

Susann Brailey   Joy Abella

Senior Editor   Administrative Editor

P.S. Look for these women's fiction titles coming in May! Multiple-award-winning and bestselling author Deborah Smith enchants us with **A PLACE TO CALL HOME;** what the *Chicago Tribune* calls "a beautiful, believable love story" is now available in paperback. When Claire Delaney returns to her childhood home in Georgia to recuperate from an accident, she realizes that her love for Roan Sullivan has not diminished through the years. A turbulent reunion takes them to their childhood haunts and forces them to overcome twenty years of pain and separation in order to make a life together for themselves. Applauded by *Romantic Times* as "truly a bright light of the genre that shines brighter with each new novel," Karyn Monk returns with **THE WITCH AND THE WARRIOR,** a Scottish romance that ingeniously combines humor and passion. And immediately following this page, preview the Bantam women's fiction titles on sale in April!

For current information on Bantam's women's fiction, visit our Web site *Isn't It Romantic?* at the following address:
http://www.bdd.com/romance

"Amanda Quick seems to be writing . . . better and better."—*Chicago Tribune*

WITH THIS RING

by *New York Times* bestselling author

Amanda Quick

Available in hardcover.

Beatrice Poole may be a vicar's daughter, but she knows enough about darker passions to have carved out a highly successful career penning "horrid novels." Now the talented authoress finds herself in the midst of an ominous adventure that rivals anything she's ever written.

Her Uncle Reggie is dead, his house has been ransacked, and Beatrice suspects he was murdered—all because of his keen interest in the Forbidden Rings of Aphrodite, said to bestow the most unnatural powers. That's why Beatrice has braved the wilds of Devon to seek out a leading authority on arcane matters: the famously eccentric, possibly dangerous Earl of Monkcrest, a man believed to dabble in the supernatural.

But bearding the Mad Monk of Monkcrest in his den may be the biggest mistake of Beatrice's life. For suddenly she finds herself joined in an uneasy alliance with a man who is every bit as fascinating as one of the heroes in her novels.

Yet the alliance won't necessarily keep her safe. For somewhere in the netherworld of London, a villain lurks, waiting for the pair to unearth the Forbidden Rings—knowing that when they do, that day will be their last.

A THIN DARK LINE

by *New York Times* bestselling
author of *Guilty as Sin*

Tami Hoag

Available in paperback.

*Terror stalks the streets of Bayou Breaux, Louisiana.
A suspected murderer is free on a technicality, and
the cop accused of planting evidence against him is
ordered off the case. But Detective Nick Fourcade
refuses to walk away. He's stepped over the line before. This case threatens to push him over the edge.*

*He's not the only one. Deputy Annie Broussard
found the woman's mutilated body. She still hears
the phantom echoes of dying screams. She wants justice. But pursuing the investigation will mean form-
ing an alliance with a man she doesn't trust and
making enemies of the men she works with. It will
mean being drawn into the confidence of a suspected
killer. For Annie Broussard, finding justice will
mean risking everything—including her life.*

*The search for the truth has begun—one that
will lead down a twisted trail through the steamy
bayous of Louisiana, and deep into the darkest
reaches of the human heart.*

Nationally bestselling author Teresa Medeiros
makes the American West her own in the new
completely captivating historical romance . . .

NOBODY'S DARLING

by Teresa Medeiros

*When pretty, young Bostonian Esmerelda Fine hears that
her brother has been killed out West, she sells everything
she owns and sets out to find her brother's murderer and
bring him to justice. But Billy Darling, the man accused of
the murder, is nothing like she expects. First of all, he's
devastatingly attractive. But second, not only does he claim
not to have killed her brother, it's beginning to look like
her brother is alive and well . . . a wanted man. When
Esmerelda hires Billy to track her brother down, the adventure, and the passion, have just begun. . . .*

Billy Darling was a jovial drunk.

Which explained the dangerous edge to his temper as he surveyed the haughty young miss who had
presumed to interrupt his poker game. His first whiskey of the day sat untouched on the table just inches
from his fingertips. The way his day was going, he
doubted it would be his last.

The woman disagreed. Noting the direction of his
glance, she gave the brimming glass an imperious
nod. "You'd best finish your whiskey, sir. It may be
the last you taste for a very long while."

Billy barely resisted the urge to bust out laughing.
Instead, he curled his fingers around the glass and
lifted it in a salute to her audacity. She really ought to
be flattered by the stir her announcement had caused.

Noreen had gone tumbling off his lap in a flurry of scarlet petticoats while Dauber and Seal went diving under a nearby table, scattering bills and coins.

Only Drew had remained upright, but even he had scooted his chair back a good two feet and thrown his hands into the air. The waxed tips of his mustache quivered with alarm. Billy suspected he would have joined the cowboys under the table if he hadn't feared rumpling the new paisley waistcoat he'd had shipped all the way from Philadelphia. You could almost always count on Drew's vanity overruling his cowardice.

It wasn't the first time Billy had faced a woman across the barrel of a gun, and it probably wouldn't be the last. Hell, he'd even been shot once by a jealous whore in Abilene. But she'd cried so prettily and tended the wound and the rest of him with such gratifying remorse, he'd forgiven her before the bleeding stopped.

It wasn't even that he particularly minded being shot by a woman. He just wanted to do something to deserve it first.

He drained the rest of the whiskey in a single searing swallow and thumped the glass to the table, making her flinch. "Why don't you put the gun down? You really don't want to get powder burns on your pretty white gloves, do you, Miss . . . ?"

"Fine. Miss Esmerelda Fine."

She flung her name at him like a challenge, but it failed to trigger even an echo of recognition. "Esmerelda? Now that's a rather lofty name for such a little bit of a lady. Suppose I just call you Esme?"

He would have thought it impossible, but her mouth grew even more pinched. "I'd rather you didn't. My brother was the only one who called me Esme." Then that same mouth surprised him by curving into a sweetly mocking smile. "Unless, of course, you'd rather I call you *Darling?*"

Billy scowled at her. "The last man who cast aspersions on my family name got a belly full of lead." In reality, he'd only gotten a bloody nose, but since Billy didn't plan to give either to this persistent young lady, he didn't see any harm in embellishing.

"It wouldn't have been my brother, by any chance, would it? Is that why you gunned down a defenseless boy? For hurting your poor, delicate feelings?"

"Ah." Billy's good humor returned as he folded his arms over his chest and tilted his chair back on two legs. "Now we're getting somewhere. Do refresh my memory, Miss Fine. You can't expect me to remember every man I'm supposed to have killed."

"I should have expected no less than such callous disregard from an animal like you, Mr. Darling. A cold-blooded assassin masquerading as a legitimate bounty hunter." Her contemptuous gaze flicked to Drew. "Sheriff, I demand that you arrest this man immediately for the murder of Bartholomew Fine III."

"What happend to the first two Bartholomews?" Dauber whispered. "Billy kill them, too?"

Seal elbowed him in the ribs, earning a sharp grunt.

Drew twirled one tip of his mustache, a habit he indulged in only in moments of great duress. "Now, lass," he purred in that lilting mixture of Scottish burr and western drawl that was so exclusively his. "There's no reason to get your wee feathers all in a ruffle. I remain confident that this private quarrel between you and Mr. Darling can be settled in a civilized manner without the discharge of firearms."

"Private quarrel?" The woman's voice rose to a near shriek. "According to that Wanted poster out there, this man is a public menace with a price on his head. I insist that you take him in!"

Drew sputtered an ineffectual retort, but Billy's melted-butter-and-molasses drawl cut right through it. "And just where do you propose he take me?"

Miss Fine blinked, her face going blank for a gratifying moment. "Why, the jail, I suppose."

Billy slanted Drew a woeful look. Avoiding Miss Fine's eyes, Drew polished his badge with his ruffled shirtsleeve. "Sorry, lass, but our jail's not equipped to hold Mr. Darling. You'll have to take your complaint to the U.S. marshal in Santa Fe."

Righting his chair, Billy favored her with a rueful grin, briefly entertaining the notion that she and her sad little bonnet just might admit defeat and creep away to let him finish his poker game in peace. After all, any fellow hapless enough to be stuck with the name of Bartholomew was probably better off dead.

She dashed his hopes by swaying forward, her voice husky with menace. "If this miserable excuse for a lawman—"

"Now wait just one minute there, lass!" Drew cried, his Scottish accent deepening along with his agitation. If she got him any more riled, there would be g's dropping and r's rolling all over the saloon. "There's no need to insult my—"

She turned the gun on him; his defense subsided to a sulky pout. She returned it to Billy, aiming it square at his heart.

"If this miserable excuse for a lawman won't take you in," she repeated firmly, "then I will. I'll take you to Santa Fe and turn you over to the U.S. marshal myself. Why, I'll hog-tie you to the back of a stagecoach and drag you all the way to Boston if I have to, Mr. Darling."

Billy sighed wearily. She'd left him with no choice but to call her bluff. As the smile faded from his eyes, the bartender vanished behind the bar, Drew inched his chair backward, and Dauber and Seal plugged their ears with their fingertips.

Billy rested his hands palms-down on the table, flexing his fingers with deceptive indolence. "Oh, yeah?" he drawled. "Who says?"

Little Miss Fine-and-Mighty cocked the derringer, her face going white with strain. "I've got one shot in this chamber that says you're coming with me."

The Colt .45 appeared in Billy's hand as if by magic, accompanied by a personable grin. "And I've got six shots in this here Colt that say I'm not."

Esmerelda stared dumbly at the gun in Darling's hand. His movements hadn't betrayed even a hint of a blur. One second his hand had been empty. The next it had been cradling an enormous black pistol. The imposing barrel dwarfed the stunted mouth of her derringer, making it look like a toy. Darling's smile was unflinching, but all traces of green had disappeared from his eyes, leaving them ruthless chips of flint.

Esmerelda sucked in a steadying breath, cringing when it caught in a squeak. She'd spent so many sleepless nights in the past few months dreaming of the moment when she would confront her brother's murderer. But none of the possible scenarios had included engaging him in a standoff. Billy Darling was rumored to be a crack shot, lethally accurate at thirty yards, much less four feet. What was the proper etiquette in these situations? Should she suggest they choose seconds? Step outside and draw at twenty paces? She flexed her numb fingers, choking back a hysterical giggle.

Almost as if he'd read her mind, he said, "It has occurred to me, Miss Fine, that this may very well be your first gunfight. We have both drawn our weapons so all that remains is to determine which one of us has the guts to pull the trigger. If you'd rather not find out, then I suggest you lay your gun on the table and back out of here. Nice and slow."

"Now, William," the sheriff whined. "You know you've never shot a woman before."

Darling's affable smile did not waver. "Nor has one ever given me cause to."

"Drop your weapon, sir," Esmerelda commanded, praying the derringer wouldn't slip out of her sweat-dampened glove. She waited a respectable interval before adding a timid,

"P-p-please."

"I asked you first."

She'd forfeited all she held dear just to come to this godforsaken town and bring her brother's killer to justice. And there he sat, smirking at her with cool aplomb, all the while knowing that he had crushed her brother's life beneath his boot heel with no more concern than for a discarded cigar butt.

Esmerelda suddenly realized that she no longer wanted justice. She wanted vengeance. Her finger tightened on the trigger. A scalding tear trickled down her cheek, then another. She dashed them away with one hand, but fresh ones sprang into their place to blur her vision.

She did not see the sheriff rock back in his chair, grinning with relief. Billy Darling might be able to stand down the meanest desperado in five territories or gun down a fleeing outlaw without blinking an eye, but he never could abide a woman's tears.

"Aw, hell, honey, don't cry. I didn't mean to scare you. . . ."

Billy was out of his seat and halfway around the table, hand outstretched, when Esmerelda Fine, who had never so much as swatted a fly without a pang of regret, closed her eyes and squeezed the trigger.

"Fresh, charming, warm and witty, Katie Rose
writes deliciously romantic stories.
I can't wait to read more of them!"
—Teresa Medeiros, nationally bestselling author

From a delightful new voice comes a totally unique
historical romance: a clever and utterly irresistible
tale of New York City in the "Age of Innocence,"
where a lady who talks to spirits discovers just how
heavenly passion can be when you add . . .

A HINT OF MISCHIEF

by Katie Rose

*For the bewitching Jennifer Appleton and her charming
sisters, there is nothing the least bit wicked about holding a
séance. The spirits the trio conjure up seem to offer the
unhappy matrons of Victorian Manhattan a great deal of
comfort . . . and after all, impoverished young ladies
have to make a living somehow. So it's something of a
shock when a darkly handsome and coldly furious stranger
shows up at their door, aiming accusations of fraud—and
his remarkably compelling gaze—at lovely, wide-eyed Jennifer.*

*Convinced she's swindled his grieving mother out of a
sizable sum, Gabriel Forester swears he'll put this brazen
conniver out of business for good. But the lady he confronts
is a total revelation—and a surprising temptation. Now, as
the fiery opponents square off, passion flares unexpectedly,
and Gabriel and Jennifer find themselves drawn into a
devilish game of seduction where they must learn to ignore*

the ghostly voices of the past . . . and listen to their hearts.

It was her. The devil herself, Jennifer Appleton. She was dressed in a pretty dotted-white-on-white Swiss chiffon, a pink sash tied just below her breasts. The dress was a little old-fashioned, but of good material and lovely styling. He had difficulty pulling his eyes away from her, for as he had supposed, her figure was magnificent. It was generously exposed by the light quality of her dress, and he surmised she wore little beneath the gown. Although the heat made such considerations practical, it was scandalous nevertheless.

When she finally lifted her face, he saw that she bloomed with color. If the fright of the lawyer's letter affected her, it was not apparent in her easy manner, her full, lush giggles, nor her joie de vivre as she swung a croquet mallet and deftly landed her ball just outside the wicket. She must have felt his observation, for her eyes met his and held him spellbound.

"Jennifer! You must come! Oh please, they are asking for you!"

A beautiful woman approached her, and Gabriel identified Jennifer's sister. Penelope led her away to a group of women clustered beneath a shade tree with their ices and fans. Gabriel recognized Mesdames Merriweather and Greyson, the Misses Billings and Miss Barry. He waited for their rebuff, but instead, they seemed genuinely pleased to meet 'The Appleton.' Their talk grew animated, and Gabriel drifted close enough to hear the conversation.

"Is it true that you brought Mary Forester's husband back from the dead? What was it like?" Eleanore Greyson asked, her stern face lit up with excitement.

"How do you do it? Can you feel the ghostly presence?" The normally reserved Margaret Merriweather questioned.

"Are you frightened, living alone, knowing that spirits have been in your house?" Jane Billings wanted to know, her voice pleading.

"How do you give such marvelous readings? I've heard of your powers from several sources!" Judith Barry gushed.

Stunned, Gabriel saw Jennifer wield her power like a queen deigning to speak with peasants. She answered their questions cleverly, making them curious for more. Idly he realized her intelligence outweighed her beauty, but more obvious was her formidable charm. That, Jennifer Appleton had in boatloads.

Incensed, Gabriel was about to accost her when Jonathan Wiseley stole up beside him, a glass of beer in one hand, a chocolate cake in the other. "Pretty girl," he remarked, chomping on the cake. "I hear she's taking New York by storm."

"What are you talking about?" Gabriel blazed, and the young man nearly choked on his beer.

"Well, didn't you know? The 'bewitching trio' has been seen everywhere. They had tea at the Billingses, lunch at the Swathmores. I hear they've been invited to every major outing this summer. No one seems to know much about them, except that their parents, who were of good family, died. Poor dears! But there's no doubt as to their success."

Gabriel saw the truth of the man's words as the women piled knee-deep to get a word with Jennifer. Far from being out of her element, she played the crowd like a conductor of an orchestra. Worse, she seemed to be enjoying herself immensely, for she fanned herself prettily, letting the heat climb in her cheeks. Soon men surrounded her, and Gabriel could hear them fighting over who would bring her a glass of punch.

"As I said, poor little orphans. I for one would certainly like to adopt one of them. Say, do you think they are free lovers like that creature Woodhull? That would be terribly convenient, wouldn't it?"

Gabriel opened his mouth to retort, but didn't trust himself to speak. For some reason, he was furious with Jonathan's comment, and even more furious with the men thronging around Jennifer. Turning rudely away from Jonathan, he approached her, and heard her trying to decide whether to attend the Adam's ball, or the Chambers Street festival, a decision she seemed to enjoy mightily.

"Miss Appleton, I beg a private word with you." Gabriel sent her a look that brooked no refusal. As the men booed, Jennifer shrugged her dainty white shoulders, then descended from the crowd. Gabriel took her by the arm and practically dragged her into the rose garden.

"Unhand me this minute!" Jennifer cried as soon as they were alone.

Gabriel released her, suddenly aware that he *was* still holding her arm. Jennifer Appleton stood in front of him amid the Barrymores' prized Silver Lace roses, looking incredibly beautiful. Instead of appearing frightened by his confrontation, she held her chin up defiantly, as if prepared to defend her ground at all costs.

She looked so adorable Gabriel had trouble staying angry. He had to remind himself of exactly who she was—and what she was. "Miss Appleton," he managed sternly, "what are you doing here? Is it common for tea-leaf readers, who bilk elderly ladies out of money, to entertain at garden parties in such a manner?"

"And what, sir, is your objection?"

He could have sworn he saw laughter lurking at the corners of her mouth. He gestured to her gown.

"I think you know exactly what I mean. That you are here, dressed like that, flaunting yourself before the men! How did you get invited to this gathering, or did you just crash the gates?"

She was so close, he could smell her lilac water, so reminiscent of the letter to Charles. She was even prettier here than at a distance, for she seemed to emanate an energy and vitality that was intoxicating. His own thoughts drove him to distraction. Part of him wanted to put her over his knee and beat some sense into her; the other part wanted to kiss her until she swooned.

"I was invited by Madame Barrymore herself, thanks to a recommendation by the Misses Billings," Jennifer said indignantly, although she didn't seem entirely displeased with the situation. "As to my dress, it is no different than Sally Vesper's gown, nor Marybeth's. And I wasn't flaunting myself; I find the company of this society very congenial. I also find *your* interest questionable, since you are here escorting a female."

He gaped at her, outraged that she should turn his questions back on him. "You are the most exasperating woman I've ever had the misfortune to meet! Do you know what they are saying about you? They think you are like Victoria Woodhull, a free lover as well as a spiritualist! Is that the reputation you want?"

"I see." She lowered her face, appearing appropriately demure, but Gabriel knew better. He could almost sense her restrained mirth. When she looked up a moment later, it was as if a halo encircled her fair head.

"I truly appreciate your concern. As a gentleman, it was most kind of you to instruct me in the error of my ways. I am reformed, sir, thanks to you. I shall be forever grateful."

With that, she rose on her pink slippers and

placed a schoolmistress-like peck on his cheek. "Good day, Mr. Forester. I leave you the garden."

Gabriel's admiration mingled with his outrage and disbelief as Jennifer daintily curtsied, then swirled to walk gracefully out of the glade. Evidently, she saw him as some mawkish schoolboy she could toy with. His thoughts went back to her legal reply to Charles's letter, to the incident with the police, even to his first confrontation with her. So far, she had bested him at every turn. He had to appreciate her audacity, even as it enraged his male ego. She badly needed a lesson, Gabriel decided. One that he would teach her.

"Miss Appleton?"

He laid his hand on her shoulder, intending to give her a well-deserved dressing down, but she turned so quickly that she wound up in his arms. The merriment disappeared from her eyes and she looked at him with something else, something that made him think she didn't entirely despise him back. His chastising words suddenly caught in his throat as he gazed into her eyes, eyes that had convinced lesser souls they'd seen a ghost. As if of its own accord, his mouth lowered to hers, unable to resist the soft, sweet temptation.

On sale in May:

A PLACE TO CALL HOME
by Deborah Smith

THE WITCH AND THE WARRIOR
by Karyn Monk

Bestselling Historical Women's Fiction

❊ AMANDA QUICK ❊

____28354-5 SEDUCTION . . .$6.50/$8.99 Canada

____28932-2 SCANDAL . . . .$6.50/$8.99

____28594-7 SURRENDER . . . .$6.50/$8.99

____29325-7 RENDEZVOUS . . . .$6.50/$8.99

____29315-X RECKLESS . . . .$6.50/$8.99

____29316-8 RAVISHED . . . .$6.50/$8.99

____29317-6 DANGEROUS . . . .$6.50/$8.99

____56506-0 DECEPTION . . . .$6.50/$8.99

____56153-7 DESIRE . . . .$6.50/$8.99

____56940-6 MISTRESS . . . .$6.50/$8.99

____57159-1 MYSTIQUE . . . .$6.50/$7.99

____57190-7 MISCHIEF . . . .$6.50/$8.99

____57407-8 AFFAIR . . . .$6.99/$8.99

❊ IRIS JOHANSEN ❊

____29871-2 LAST BRIDGE HOME . . .$5.50/$7.50

____29604-3 THE GOLDEN

                     BARBARIAN . . . .$6.99/$8.99

____29244-7 REAP THE WIND . . . . . .$5.99/$7.50

____29032-0 STORM WINDS . . . .$6.99/$8.99

Ask for these books at your local bookstore or use this page to order.

Please send me the books I have checked above. I am enclosing $____ (add $2.50 to cover postage and handling). Send check or money order, no cash or C.O.D.'s, please.

Name _____

Address _____

City/State/Zip _____

Send order to: Bantam Books, Dept. FN 16, 2451 S. Wolf Rd., Des Plaines, IL 60018
Allow four to six weeks for delivery.
Prices and availability subject to change without notice.   FN 16 3/98

Bestselling Historical Women's Fiction

⚔ IRIS JOHANSEN ⚔

____28855-5 THE WIND DANCER . . .$5.99/$6.99
____29968-9 THE TIGER PRINCE . . .$6.99/$8.99
____29944-1 THE MAGNIFICENT
ROGUE . . . .$6.99/$8.99
____29945-X BELOVED SCOUNDREL $6.99/$8.99
____29946-8 MIDNIGHT WARRIOR . .$6.99/$8.99
____29947-6 DARK RIDER . . . .$6.99/$8.99
____56990-2 LION'S BRIDE . . . .$6.99/$8.99
____56991-0 THE UGLY DUCKLING. . .$5.99/$7.99
____57181-8 LONG AFTER MIDNIGHT.$6.99/$8.99
____10616-3 AND THEN YOU DIE.... $22.95/$29.95

⚔ TERESA MEDEIROS ⚔

____29407-5 HEATHER AND VELVET .$5.99/$7.50
____29409-1 ONCE AN ANGEL . . . . . .$5.99/$7.99
____29408-3 A WHISPER OF ROSES .$5.99/$7.99
____56332-7 THIEF OF HEARTS . . . . .$5.50/$6.99
____56333-5 FAIREST OF THEM ALL .$5.99/$7.50
____56334-3 BREATH OF MAGIC . . . .$5.99/$7.99
____57623-2 SHADOWS AND LACE . . .$5.99/$7.99
____57500-7 TOUCH OF
ENCHANTMENT. . . . .$5.99/$7.99

Ask for these books at your local bookstore or use this page to order.

Please send me the books I have checked above. I am enclosing $____ (add $2.50 to cover postage and handling). Send check or money order, no cash or C.O.D.'s, please.

Name _____

Address _____

City/State/Zip _____

Send order to: Bantam Books, Dept. FN 16, 2451 S. Wolf Rd., Des Plaines, IL 60018
Allow four to six weeks for delivery.
Prices and availability subject to change without notice.   FN 16 3/98